Alfie's Sock
and Other Stories

by
Robbie Laughton

ALFIE'S SOCK

With the manual Contented Little Baby opened, the bath water tested safe with an elbow and Alfie, only three days old, was gently half submerged. Screaming. There was nothing in the text regarding that. When awake, no matter what, Alfie screamed. What were we doing wrong? He was a long baby, as the midwife described. Years later, we learned that breast milk may not have been nourishing enough and instead of being colic, Alfie may have been hungry. By chance, we discovered that he became a contented little baby when taken for long walks in the pram. He would stare at rolling fluffy clouds, tops of trees and the upper deck of the number 73 bus as it passed by on Islington High Street, kicking with excitement until he was worn out. Then he slept.

One morning during a sunny walk up and down the streets lined with Victorian and Edwardian houses Alfie was very active. Enough so that he looked hot. His blanket, baby cap and socks were carefully placed in the rack underneath the pram. Returning through the tall gate at the side of our house to our garden flat, he was picked up and placed on his exercise mattress on the living room floor. The poppers of his baby-grow were slowly released, and he lay in his nappy asleep. His clothes were folded and placed on the table. But there was only one stripey sock. It didn't matter. Socks had been a popular present that month from visiting friends and family.

Shrieks of a wailing urban fox, resembling a screaming baby, woke the neighbourhood. Bedroom windows were slammed as the fox scurried in the shadows from bin to bin in search of fast food. Foxes were the litter bugs in the area, scavenging for any leftovers, scattering rubbish over pavements and gardens. A group of neighbours fed up with the trauma and potential harm from these 'scraggy creatures' had clubbed together and illegally hired gunmen armed with silenced air rifles to crawl the streets at night and rid them of the 'pests' to no effect. The ripped off neighbours returned to emailing the council en masse.

A pregnant vixen sniffed a bench in Gibson Square. The rays of street lights were broken by the swaying leaves of a Sycamore. Something interested her. Standing on her hind legs she stealthily stretched her nose to the arm of the bench. It was the scent of a baby that had attracted her to Alfie's sock that had been placed, by a hopeful person, for a parent to find. Startled by the sound of voices the vixen slid away into the shadows. A couple approached and they were arguing ascending into a proper row. She was screaming, "I fucking hate you!" repeatedly. His arms held her shoulders as he shouted in her face, "You fucking bitch!" Crack! She slapped him across his face and attempted to scratch his eyes out. He pushed the screaming woman just enough to land a blow to her nose which burst with blood on impact.

"Hey! Hey! What do you think you're doing!" a man shouted running out of one of the terraced houses opposite the square, "Are you alright? Are you alright?" The girl was on her knees, hands on face, covered in blood.

The boyfriend looked round, "And who the fuck are you! That bitch's knight in shining armour?" and smashed the neighbour with a Tyson punch enough to knock him to the floor. The girlfriend got up and kicked the neighbour in the face shouting, "Let's do the fucker!" A few more kicks from the couple left the knight in shining armour unconscious. The girl and boyfriend shuffled away as the beam of headlights from a black cab came from around the corner. The vixen oblivious to human conflict, snook passed the cab driver who was knelt above the neighbour on the side of the road, and snatched Alfie's sock from the bench.

Andover Estate was a police no go area, known as Beirut in Islington. A warren of alleyways made it impossible for policing. But the vixen knew her way around and returned to her den, a hidden hole at the side of a row of lock-ups. Her safe place. As daylight broke, the vixen picked up her cub by the scruff of its neck, who had been playing with Alfie's sock behind the dustbins. Both went into hiding.

A gang of youths in school uniform were huddled by the lock-ups, all eyes peering at something. One of the boys was proudly presenting his new toy to his mates. A throwing knife glistened in his hand. That area was heavily involved in postcode wars, where youths had found themselves voluntarily or involuntarily involved. N7 3HU was a battleground and blood had been shed on numerous occasions, more recently with another teenage death. Kids as young as ten were carrying knives to school for protection. Metal detectors had been installed on school entrances without success. Stabbings still occurred. The boys took turns throwing the knife at the wooden post of a sign stating NO BALL GAMES. One boy who went looking for a target from overflowing bins, hung Alfie's sock to the post on a rusty bent tack. In turn they threw the knife, spinning it towards the stripy sock until they grew bored of missing the target and continued on their walk to school. Knife hidden under the hard base of a Nike holdall.

Gusts of wind blew plastic bags in swirls around the estate, and Alfie's sock fell from the post to the hard mud beneath, where it lay throughout the day. That evening, a man with a Staffordshire Bull Terrier, eyes glued to his Blackberry with both thumbs tapping away, was led by the dog zig-zagging along the pavement following its nose. The dog cocked its leg on the no ball games signpost, sniffed around the mud and continued to zig-zag carrying Alfie's sock locked in its teeth. Tapping his card on the rear of the busy number 30 night-bus, the dog heaved itself up the steps to the upper deck. With a glance at mainly occupied seats, jumped next to its master on its second attempt, out of breath. His face was still buried in his phone. Three stops later by the charity shop, lads in sportswear flagged the bus down carrying a softball bat and two heavy plastic bags over their shoulders, and clambered upstairs and occupied the back seats. Totally intoxicated. A stocky lad pulled a black high heeled shoe from one of the bags, held high above his head, and in a well spoken accent he addressed the bus load of people, "Ladies and gentlemen. Would anyone like a pair of shoes? We have a wide range of footwear worthy of royalty going to a good pair of feet. Just observe the quality. Here madam, please try this for size. And for your boyfriend, here's a pair of suede boots worthy of a king." More shoes were pulled from the charity bags and held up high then tossed about the upper deck to random onlookers. Most roared with laughter as footwear was thrown from the back of the bus to whoever raised their hands. Heckled by some, for shoes being odd sizes or different colours, what could have been a boring journey home was hilarious. The Staffy watched every throw and decided that leather was better than a striped sock and began to chase the trajectory of each shoe playfully, occasionally being teased before the dog legged it down the aisle jumping over seats of people to sink its teeth into shoes. Still on his Blackberry and uninterested in the endeavours of his dog or the spontaneous participation of travellers on the night-bus, he walked down the aisle, patted his thigh, to signal that they were getting off. Dutifully, the Staffy followed. Congratulated with applause, the dog, brogue in its mouth, awkwardly jumped off the bus following the heels of its master. Trodden and kicked by trampling feet on the deck of the bus for hours, eventually Alfie's sock landed in a gutter gushing with rain water, by the side of a McDonald's carton caught by a bundle of twigs and fag butts.

Once a practising dentist and happily married father of twins, the drills and spills of dentistry had taken its toll and Brian now cleaned the roads of Islington, driving a council road sweeper. Not only did his marriage break down, he did also, losing access to his children and finally found himself sectioned and in rehab for the best part of a year. He enjoyed keeping the streets of his borough clean and felt that he was positively making the world a better place. It had been raining the night before, and waste had collected in the gutter. Certain care had to be applied to gather the dams of debris. Brian was meticulous, and would rather reverse if anything was missed than get back 20 minutes early having completed his route. Among the twigs and gathered cartons, Alfie's sock was whisked up by Brian's brushes, flung into the rotors and carried, twisted on the filthy mechanism, down Essex Road.

Saturday lunch times were always buzzing in Islington when Arsenal had a home game especially when it was a local derby or when Manchester United visited. Most pubs within walking distance from Highbury had a strict HOME FANS ONLY policy with a few exceptions. A coach load of Manchester United fans had discovered that The Dog and Dumpling served Stella on draught and offered basic pub grub on polystyrene plates with a wooden fork. It was three hours before kick off and these lads were already smashed, lobbing chips at each other until they were politely asked to stop or eat outside. Game on. Chips were flying everywhere, mushy peas rubbed in faces and pints in flimsy plastic thrown at each other. The patron had seen this all before, and had a wry smile on his face being a secret United fan living in London. One lad had his face and Fred Perry t-shirt caked in beans, and went into the lounge to wipe himself clean with a beer towel from the bar. On his return, his pint had a foreign object in it to the amusement of his mates. Alfie's sock was submerged, overflowing with froth, and subsequently became the object of humour being tossed about, leaving damp patches on any innocent turned back. The sound of 'United! United!' was heard, and they were joined by even more away fans. The sock game stopped. Northern voices joined forces as they marched together, hands clapping in unison, towards the stadium.

A blind man tapped his stick down North Church Rd heading towards the row of shops. A well rehearsed route, one that he had taken for many years. The pavement became sticky to his feet with the familiar smell of stale beer. Yet he hesitated. He traced the shape of a baby's sock. He picked up Afie's sock on the end of his stick, and gently placed it on the pub wall.

Alfie was screaming as he was pushed in the pram through the garden gate for yet another stroll around the streets. An attempt to soothe him and hopefully encourage sleep. It was Sunday after all. One block. Two blocks. Alfie was falling asleep. On our return, there on the pub wall, barely recognisable, faded and stained, was Alfie's sock.

"Hey! Alfie! Look what daddy has found! It's your lost sock!" One day, I thought, I'll write a story about Alfie's sock. But now we've got to go home and finish packing. We're moving out of London tomorrow to live in a village in the country.

HAIRY FAIRY

10.00am

Richard Hayley QC described me as a ruthless drug lord who had ruled the UK branch of a multi-million pound empire with an iron fist. I was untouchable and infamous. Twelve years, five months and twenty seven days in HMP Nottingham. My local City. And now it's my release day. Never thought today would come.

10.00am

Action For Healthy Kids. Come on. Any loose change please. Thank you Sir. Action For Healthy Kids. Loose change please. Thank you. Thank you very much. No change. I'll still be here when you've finished your shopping. I'll be here. Action For Healthy Kids.

10.50am

Sitting in this stinking release holding cell with four other inmates, all avoiding my eye contact. Nobody speaks. They're scared of me. In alphabetical order we are released. I'll be last out. What's a few hours more when you've spent over twelve years banged up. Jangling of keys and one more scumbag is set free.

10.53am

I've got to know faces in Nottingham centre over the years. They certainly know me. Dressed in my pink ballerina outfit. Helps when you're collecting for charity. I was in the Nottingham Post last year. Headline 'Hairy Fairy donates

£100,000 to charity'. That's how the name stuck. It's now my identity. People find it hilarious and remember me.

11.50am

Twelve years ago, I ran four Ferraris, worth £140,000 each, and five Porsches. Car dealers knew me so well I had a "triple A status" credit rating and I was on first name terms with my bank manager. And I had an underground garage full of guns.

11.50am

Always lived a quiet life really. Never wanted for much. Terraced house in Sneinton by the City centre. When my father went into care, he gave me his old car. Good runaround he said. He didn't use it much. Nor did I, just for supermarket runs. It was parked on the street most of the week. Action For Healthy Kids. Any change please.

11.55am

I'd passed on most of the cars with access to hidden cash for boys on the payroll to keep up repayments, get rid, or upgrade. It was important to keep my status even though I'm inside. They might have confiscated half a million pounds of my assets and eighty grand in cash, but I'll be driving a new Ferrari later today. Don't you worry.

11.56am

I was an English teacher for over twenty years. Married. But not happily. She wanted more than I could offer. Blamed me for most things. Just buried myself in my work and ignored her nagging. Action For Healthy Kids. Come on. Any loose change please. Thank you. Action For Healthy Kids.

01.50pm

My daughter is eighteen next week. Lovely girl. Paid for her boarding school every year. Cash. Hidden cash just for her. One of my boys would rock up at her school with a wad of notes at the start of every term. She never wanted for anything. Only the best for my kid. Another scumbag leaves the holding cell.

01.55pm

We didn't have kids. That might have bonded us together. My fault, she claimed. Loose change please. Action For Healthy Kids. Thank you.

02.18pm

My poor girl. Lost the use of her legs when some drunken bastard knocked her down nine years ago. She wasn't even ten. Loved ballet dancing. She was good. Apparently. Never saw her dance. Had photos of her on my wall performing. Since the accident, her photos became headshots. My wife thought it best that I didn't see the wheelchair. Best not to have a constant reminder on my cell wall.

02.20pm

Came home from work one day to find that my wife had gone. Packed all her stuff. Left a note on the kitchen table. 'You know it wasn't working but you weren't brave enough to say so. Bye.' And that was that. Gone. Action For Healthy Kids. Any change please.

03.25pm

Frank's picking me up. One of the boys. He's loyal to me and I've looked after him. Kept him out of prison even though some of the others weren't so lucky after we were busted in the car park of Annesley Working Men's Club with a suitcase of heroin. If it wasn't for him, I'd have been up for murder too. Some yardie scumbag was getting too big for his boots. Totally covered for me. Got rid of the guns whilst I was being interrogated, and any traces of me being connected to a shooting the week before in St. Annes. Frank did a total clean up with no strings.

03.30pm

Started drinking. It soon became a habit. Then a disease. It took over me. I had no friends to turn to. Nobody to share my burden. So I just drank myself to sleep. Then it became noticeable at work that I was deeply depressed. It was   affecting   my   teaching.

04.35pm

Kept myself trim over the years inside. Probably fitter and healthier now than when I was sent down. Healthy body, healthy mind and all that.

04.35pm

Finally, I was asked to take time off, to sort myself out. Come back when I was better. They seemed sympathetic and wanted to help me through my situation. I fell deeper into a dark hole. I had an accident. In the car. I didn't mean to. It all happened in a flash. But it was bad. Very bad. And I was arrested. Loose change please. Action For Healthy Kids. Thank you.

04.50pm

Last but not least. I'm out of here after twelve years, five months and twenty seven days in HMP Nottingham. I'm handed a box with my belongings. My Rolex. Three gold rings, one heavily studded with diamonds with matching cufflinks. The large steel door opened. It was hailing as I took my first steps of freedom. I can see Frank. Standing by a brand new black Land Rover with tinted windows. Out of the freezing cold into a warm top of the range motor. Lovely.

04.50pm

Any more for Action For Healthy Kids before I catch the bus home. Small change please. Thank you. You can catch me on my round tonight. Usual route. Loose change please. Action For Healthy Kids. Thank you very much. Right. Off to the bus stop. Tonight should be better. I like collecting on nights. People chat and they're more generous.

04.55pm
You know where to take me Frank. Let's have the best meal in town. I'm starving. Afterwards, we have a quick job to do. You got what I asked for? Good. Then off to see the missus. It's been a long time.

04.56pm
Frozen pizza and cup of tea chilling by the gas fire. A snooze. Then I'm ready for the evening round collecting in City centre pubs.

06.45pm
Now I'm ready. Drive to George Street and park up. We'll wait   there.

06.55pm
Usual route round Hockley then onto Lace Market. Same route every week. Collecting in twenty or so pubs and bars. Even get stopped in the street to hand me cash. It's freezing tonight. Stopped hailing though. Getting used to being cold dressed in my ballerina outfit after all these years. People like it. The colder it is, the more they give. I can hear them as I enter pubs with my collecting box. "Here he is, Hairy Fairy with his collection box. Like clockwork."

07.14pm

There he is. Like clockwork. Walking towards us. Ready Frank.

07.14pm

I saw the black Range Rover. A shudder went down my spine.

07.14pm

I opened the door. Stood in front of him and showed my gun tucked in my suit trousers. Oi. Hairy Fairy bastard. Get in the car.

07.15pm

I knew this day would come. Two armed men forcing me onto the back seat of a blacked out Land Rover. I knew who it was, and why I was taken hostage. I was a dead man.

07.15pm

You know why you're here. I've been waiting nine years for this. You drunk driving bastard.

07.15pm

I've done my time! I was sent down for five years! And I've done exactly what you said I had to.

07.15pm
You only did three years, you bastard. My daughter can't walk. Never again. For the rest of her life. She was a child when you hit her. Drunk in your car. You maimed her for life.

07.16pm
I'm sorry. I'm sorry. There isn't a day I don't think about…

07.16pm
Shut the fuck up. She was a little girl who loved dancing. Ballet dancing. And you! You drunken bastard, took that away from her. I put the gun to his head and I watch his eyes close awaiting what's next. I let him feel the tension.

07.18pm
Please! Please don't… I've worn this ballet dress and collected money for a children's charity every day for the last five years. Just as your man told me to. I've done it. I'm the Hairy Fairy of Nottingham. Everyone knows me… everyone knows I've done it.

07.18pm
And you will continue to do so for the rest of your life you bastard. Like my daughter will be in a wheelchair. Forever. Pay the price, or you're a dead man! Now fuck off !!!

07.19pm
I stand there shaking on the pavement in my ballerina dress. My collecting box is thrown from the window onto the pavement.

07.19pm
Get fucking collecting. You 'Hairy Fairy' drunken bastard. Frank. Drive me to the missus. It's time.

07.35pm
Action For Healthy Kids. Any spare change…

HAIRY FAIRY RETURNS

03.21 / 19.10.2022

Can't sleep. Most nights I can't sleep. I think of that gun being pointed at my head in the back of the Land Rover two years ago and the threat of having to continue to be Hairy Fairy and collect money every day. I can't go on like this.

11.15 / 19.10.2022

Enough is enough. I have to negotiate. Somehow change this contract on my head and become free again. I did my time inside, and spent seven years dressed as Hairy Fairy in a ballerina dress collecting money. Since my father died, I've been living off my inheritance but I want to lead a normal life. Get back to work. Teach again.

15.31 / 19.10.2022

Big Dean has built up his empire again and no doubt up to no good. I've seen him drive through the City centre in his flash Ferrari looking smug. How can he be at large again? It's not fair. I know his business in West Bridgford. A double glazing company. But that's just a facade for his dirty, evil work. But it's the only place I know I can find Big Dean to talk to him.

17.10 / 19.10.2022

I decide to drive to West Bridgford. To be brave, and speak to Big Dean.

17.35 / 19.10.2022

Parked just down the road I walk towards the store. There's a few cars in the car park and one which I recognise. It's the black Land Rover that his sidekick drives. Frank. I bottle it. Remembering my experience when I thought I was going to die. Back to my car. Trembling. I return home.

19.50 / 19.10.2022

Come on! Come on! Be brave. Don't let these bastards get the better of me.

04.10 / 20.10.2022

Still haven't managed to sleep. I have to man up. Be brave and face Big Dean. It has to be today. I can't live like this anymore.

17.05 / 20.10.2022

I drive back to West Bridgford. On approaching Big Dean's store I see the Land Rover followed by a Ferrari drive out of the car park. I decide to follow them. The Land Rover takes a left but the Ferrari continues through the City and takes a right on Woodborough Rd. I hang back in traffic. Through Mapperley, onto Plains Road. I keep my distance. It's dark which helps. Only my headlights could be seen. The Ferrari takes a sharp right towards Woodborough Village. It's now open countryside. Half way down the hill the Ferrari slows down. Large double gates open and the car disappears, and they slowly close as I pass.

17.27 / 20.10.2022

I turn my car around and drive back towards the gates. Through the hedges get a glimpse of the Ferrari parked in the courtyard of a mansion lit by security lights. Just beyond on the opposite side is a farmer's track leading to a field. I reverse my car onto the track and gather my composure.

17.41 / 20.10.2022

I get out of the car. Take a few deep breaths and walk towards the double gates. As I approach I can see an intercom system on the gatepost. I hold my hand out, pausing for a few seconds before I press the button. I hear the front door of the mansion open and a woman's voice shouting. The sound of electronic locks on a car being opened. More shouting and I can clearly hear what the woman is saying. "You can't change Dean. You're not prepared to. You're destroying me. And I've had enough. We're off." A young lady in a wheelchair appears and the woman helps her into the back of a white Range Rover. Above the revving of the engine I hear Big Dean shout "Well... fuck off then! Both of you." I quickly hide in the hedgerow as the gates open. The Range Rover speeds out of the courtyard and up the hill. The gates close slowly. I hear the front door of the mansion being slammed. Tonight is not the night to negotiate with BIg Dean.

07.50 / 21.10.2022

A good night's sleep. First time for ages. I'm feeling less anxious now. I'm making some progress, small steps towards negotiating with Big Dean. I will return tonight.

19.22 / 21.10.2022

Returning to the farmer's track, I turn the engine off. It's dark. As I was about to walk to the double gates, there's headlights and Porsche pulls up. The gates open and it enters the courtyard. Then the black Land Rover enters before the gates close. Half a minute later two more cars drive through the gates and three menacing looking men go to the front door. There's something going down I tell myself. Returning to my car, I wait and observe.

19.17 / 21.10.2022

Another car arrives and pulls up at the gates. A man gets out and presses the button of the intercom. He's holding what looks like a takeaway meal. An UberEats logo is lit by the security lights on the side of the vehicle. The gates open and the food is handed over. The gates close slowly. I need to speak to Big Dean alone. In front of his gang members there's no way I can negotiate with him. I will return tomorrow.

19.15 / 22.10.2022

Parked on the farmer's track, lights and engine off, I look at the double gates. Again the Land Rover, Porsche and two other cars arrive and enter the courtyard. And again an UberEats takeaway is delivered shortly afterwards and handed over by a woman. I get frustrated. Tomorrow. It has to be tomorrow.

19.21 / 23.10.2022

There's already the Porsche in the courtyard as the Land Rover arrives, followed by the two other cars. And shortly after an UberEats pulls up and a different man hands over the takeaway. I return home.

22.10 / 21.10.2022

Negotiating with Big Dean isn't going to plan. He's ruthless and a coldhearted killer. Now that his wife has left him. He'll be even more evil. Just go home.

04.11 / 22.10.2022
That's it. I've got it. That has to be the plan. Time to sleep now.

09.36 / 22.10.2022
Go online and apply to be an UberEats driver.

14.20 / 25.10.2022
Application for UberEats has been accepted. Tonight's the night.

18.30 / 22.10.2022
Waiting in Woodborough village. There's only two takeaways that use UberEats. A Chinese and an Indian.

18.54 / 22.10.2022
I let a couple of deliveries go. It's not Big Dean's address. Bingo! Delivery for Big Dean. I quickly accept and I'm picking up a takeaway meal for Big Dean from the Indian. It's not that heavy. Up the hill towards the double gates. I can see the Ferrari and a Porsche in the courtyard as I press the buzzer. I'm nervous. I put my hood up and look down as the gates open and the food is handed over.

18.50 / 23.10.2022
It's another takeaway delivery for Big Dean. This one is much heavier than yesterday's. Off up the hill to the double gates. There's more cars in the courtyard. It's a different man who receives the food.

18.57 / 23.10.2022
This time it's a Chinese takeaway. The bag is very light.

19.09 / 23.10.2022
Only the Ferrari is in the courtyard. It's Big Dean who's coming towards the gates as they open slowly. Head down and nervous, I hand over the bag. No words were exchanged.

19.13   /   23.10.2022
Driving home. I think of my father. Our family home where I grew up. And the tall banjo barometer that hung on the wall in the hallway. He always told me never to touch it. That the liquid in the thermometer was Thallium and highly poisonous. Online research stated that one drop of Thallium on the skin or ingested was enough to make you seriously ill. Three drops was enough to kill a person. A painful and horrible death. Virtually untraceable in autopsy. Odds are that Big Dean will have at least half a dozen drops in his body by now. Thanks to my father's old banjo barometer, and a false identity with UberEats.

Goodbye Big Dean. Goodbye Hairy Fairy.

FAT MAN TO IRONMAN

If anyone asks where it all began, I always roll out with the story of the village race. Drinking had always been close to heart, especially with other people who were well up for it too. We were a little late for a dinner party. At home, Jen shouted above the hairdryer for me to wear something decent. We had been invited to our new 'posh' friends who lived at the big house opposite the church. We'd recently moved from bustling Islington to a tranquil, highly desirable Hertfordshire village with our two young children. Due to the amount of vodka I had been necking, I was well on the way. I put on a pair of old white painters dungarees bearing splats and a blond Madonna wig. We turned up at the front door looking like we'd been arguing. To my pleasure, the night unfolded into generous consumption. For some blurry pissed reason in the early hours, we decided to draw straws for forfeits. The loser to unfold scrunched up balls of paper with the following scribbled:

Take colonic irrigation
Stand for the Parish Council
Host an art exhibition
Have   six   orgasms   at   work   in   one   day
Enter the annual village race

The Village Race was the one people feared the most, taking place the next day. Drawing the short straw, I began to unfold my forfeit revealing the letter 'V'. The village race.

Still drunk, I was encouraged to line up with the other athletes, children, mums and dads and their pet dogs. Hundreds of local villagers, made up of real locals and the new generation of London commuters, awaited the start of the 108th around the village race. Bang. Lungs on fire, I gasped for air. It felt and looked like I was running on the spot. A style that made me travel further up and down, than go forwards. Sixteen and a half stones going up and down, up and down, up and bloody down, in ratio to half a yard forwards. We weren't even at the turning of the dairy farm, less than half a mile down the country road, when two fat bottomed ladies enjoying a good chin wag, went steadily passed. Not long after, I was amongst toddlers holding the hands of parents, trotting and skipping. I was knackered. Now bringing up the rear, I turned the corner of the recreation ground for the final 100m. The crowd erupted. All faces were laughing at me, or so it felt. None more so than the bunch from the previous night's dinner party, my girlfriend and kids, rolling with laughter. I crossed the line. Last. This experience caused me to think. Early the next morning, I arose positively and ran the block. Barely a mile, it sparked the beginning of many miles to come.

I couldn't blame her really but spoken words hurt all the same. After eleven years, nine months and god knows how many days, Jen told me that she didn't fancy me anymore. Didn't fancy me. I knew she didn't. The Sunday night fear of Monday that night was combined with something deeper. It was the lowest moment. The kids were asleep, Jen was asleep and I was alone in a huge state of emotional stress and contemplation. The next morning sat alone in the drizzle on platform four in Stevenage station, watching the trains to Kings Cross come and go. I just couldn't face getting on. Unusual for me, I was going to be late for work. Little did I know at the time, I would break four hours racing Stevenage marathon in my sixth marathon the following year. On the Stevenage platform I was lost with no incentive in my life anymore. Having to force myself to work helped in a way. Dealing with emotional breakdown doesn't mean the world should stand still, waiting to pick myself up. It doesn't. Someone on every train, every morning is suffering in a quiet way. Deal with it and hurt inside. Nobody really cares.

My short term fix to be desirable again was an embarrassment. The following Saturday, as a family, we went to London for the day. It was a stark reminder that keeping a family together is bigger than a couple's relationship. Our kids found galleries uninspiring and Soho much more fascinating. I asked Jen to look after the kids for ten minutes whilst I popped into a shop on Old Compton St. Later that night when Jen and I were alone I revealed a package. Jen wasn't that impressed with the big black rubber vibrator, the latex stockings or the stimulating clitoris cream that the shop assistant said would work wonders for our relationship. What was I thinking, 'Right, this should sort everything out. Ann Summers, thank you!' I suppose it was some kind of start, maybe the realisation it wasn't a sprint, it was a hilly marathon and I had to work much harder with our relationship.

'Wonderwall' and Liam Gallagher sticks to the back of my mind, like treacle on a terracotta floor. God knows how many years since its release but I still find myself 'being Liam' when absolutely trollied. It wasn't quite Wembley Arena but a sad old night club, at the back end of Hitchin town, on a Saturday night. I'd had a skinful and my parker pockets were stacked with various flavoured vodka shots in little plastic bottles. 'Wonderwall' was crudely mixed with

'Everyone's Kung Fu Fighting'. Hands held behind my back, chin stuck out, I became 'Liam' again, front and centre on a dance platform. Later when 'The Lion Sleeps Tonight' hit our ears, I also became an elephant. Not that Liam and elephants have anything in common, more of a reflection of the state of my mind after the fourteenth sugary fruit vodka kicked in. Beyond being cool… the parker went on back to front, face covered by the hood with my right arm waving about as a trunk. Always a winner with the girlfriend.

Wasn't quite the perfect preparation for my first half marathon, but I only decided to run it on the way back, smashed in the cab. We had previously parked the car in the town centre, and I piss-talked myself into running back 14.7 miles from our village the next morning to pick it up. It was only four times longer than anything I had done before, but hey, I was well up for it. To this day I can't quite remember exactly the route I took, nor can I remember the first few miles due to my hangover. Getting lost, I decided to go cross country as the crow flies. And why was I carrying a large empty lemonade bottle in my rucksack? Must have drunk it early on the run and forgotten. So dehydrated I had to fill up in a stream. After five miles my legs were on fire and my hangover was heaving. I wondered whether I was hitting 'The Wall' but I think I hit that falling down the stairs in the club as an elephant. Three and a half hours of less jogging and more walking. I nearly passed out when I reached the car and had to wait twenty minutes until the dizziness subsided before phoning home to shout 'F*CKING DID IT!' on the answer phone. Nobody listened to the message, apart from me on my return seeing the red flashing light.

Shock to the body. That's my opinion of what happened. Everyone had a theory but nobody had an answer for nearly three months. I was running all right, now in the direction of the nearest loo. My arse was squirting as soon as I put food to my lips. Even when my bowels weren't erupting and churning with pain, I could still shit through the eye of a needle from a yard away. I was getting good at aiming at the toilet, standing up, stinking the whole place out. I wasn't well. After a few days, I changed my diet to omit heavy fats. Then after a couple of weeks, more concerned I visited my local GP. That didn't help. I was getting so concerned by now, I didn't give a squirt what people thought. Commuters spotted books I was reading on the train, titles like 'DON'T SHIT THE BED!'. I had shit the bed a few times. A simple fart became total chaos. My kids soon realised that climbing into daddy's bed in the middle of the night was worse than their nightmare.

All this went on for weeks, months. I thought I would never do a solid dump or a long satisfying fart ever again. Still kept up the training though for the London Marathon. I was running more than ever. The worst thing I had to go through, apart from rolls and rolls of bog paper, was the 'stop running' advice everyone was giving. Whether it was the cause of the shits or not, I wasn't going to stop running. Not now. I hated the situation I was in, but I hated being three and a half stones heavier and totally unfit. I had become thin but not healthy. I looked f*cking terrible, nobody could deny it. My face was gaunt and my frame looked like that of a malnourished junky. I had disappeared. Clothes hung off me like a child experimenting in a fancy dress box full of grannies old clothes. What was even harder to handle, people blanked me, not knowing who the f*ck I was. It became somewhat embarrassing for me and for them. I remember a girl at college in my first year who looked unbelievable dressed in leather and studs, caked in heavy seductive make-up. After we copped together, we arranged to meet later in the week. I went round to her bedsit and knocked on the door, only to find her flat mate. Or who I thought was her flat mate. It was my date without her make-up and clobber. Awkward. I was inflicting the same awkwardness on everybody now. Close friends, colleagues and clients who I had not seen for a while, didn't recognise me. "Is that Robbie?"

Arriving at Silverstone at the crack of dawn for the half marathon, I realised that this might be more difficult than I had anticipated. Imagine ten thousand runners queuing for stinking cubicles with joggers shits, and me at the back of the queue already with a wet gusset from the journey. At least now I was amongst others who, temporarily, were in the same boat as me. It felt normal, for a while. However, they were able to eat the pre-race banana and fill up on high five carbo drinks. This made me envious and more nervous. My target was to break 2 hours. Now that doesn't sound a lot to marathon runners but we all start somewhere. To make things even more stressful, I had the added pressure of racing with my running partner. Paul hadn't run more than about 8 miles but was well up for a half and breaking two hours. We all lined up on the formula one track ready for the gun, pre race nerves fluttered through the lycra clad crowd (and my guts). Too late for me, I had already shit my pants a couple of times. Off we went at an 1500m pace round the most boring monotonous route you could imagine. A flat concrete track, grass verges with stacks of tyres here and there perfectly placed for crashes (and my light brown liquid). That's where I lost Paul. I tried to run hard but my energy levels were too low. I was desperate to catch up in fear of being beaten. What if he breaks two hours and I don't? That was the case. I checked my Garmin and pushed it as hard as possible. My finish time: two hours and 2 seconds. 'Shit' was all I could say.

Never again. The first words out of my breathless body after crossing the finish line at Ironman UK- swimming 2.4 miles in open water, cycling 112 miles around undulating Dorset and then running a marathon. I was f*cked big time. The commentator blasted my name and a minimal biog over the tannoy in a Canadian accent. He had been bleating in the distance afternoon as finishers crossed the line. The medal hung around my son's neck and the T-shirt drowned my four year old daughter. My sister was concerned and handed me a burger. I was chuffed though. It was an achievement and a half, and I had done it. Not quite the same as saving someone's life or giving birth, but all the same, at that moment it felt like both combined.

The final mile of the ironman marathon is special. Adrenaline kicks in and you enjoy the crowds cheering you on. My last mile, I found my head had caved in. An inner voice had been telling me to stop long before that, and my muscles had been aggressively arguing with pain for hours. That's all part of it and I was well trained to cope. But something weird happened when I was running alone on the dual carriage, the fear came. I couldn't handle finishing in front of thousands of people. More to the point I didn't think I could face my family and friends. What's that about? Mind games now and so near the thrilling finish. I'd trained hard to the manual and had huge amounts of emotional and physical support for the best part of a year. Why now? How many times had I got the fear on a Sunday night after a weekend caning alcohol. How many times had I got the fear seconds before a terrifying pitch in a glassed meeting room in a corporate tower full of peering suits, but handled it. My tank was on zero mentally and physically. I was wasted. My engine had burnt itself to pieces. Only one mile to go. Stop. Just stop, that's all you have to do. Stop.

But you can't…

Sixteen years later after completing my first ironman, seven across Europe, The Norseman (the toughest triathlon in the world) and representing GB in my age group category in Australia, cycling from Lands End to John 'O' Groats and Paris to Nice, having raced for a year at the velodrome and National grasstrack events, climbed The Three Peaks Challenge in under 24 hours with my son, I'm now back to square one. 'Fatman to Ironman to Fatman.' And single (fat had nothing to do with that, but that's another story). Time for a pint.

LOCKED DOWN STUDENTS

Tom Zenetti's 'You Want Me' blasted from speakers around midnight, as three security officers armed with cameras barged in our dimmed common room. More than thirty of us flew out of the fire exit, scrambling through bushes, leaving music linked to an iphone playlist behind. The music stopped. "Someone's trampled on a rabbit. It's quivering!" a girl shrieked. "You lot injured it!" security shouted into the darkness, as the rabbit was put out of its misery.

Let's put this in context. This wouldn't have happened before covid. Student life had dramatically changed. We believed that the 'best time of our lives' would be spent at Uni, but we're now living in severe lockdown. That rabbit would still be alive, and we would have been off our trollies at 'The Warehouse' until three. We were now living in a policed society on campus, constantly being scrutinised by Uni staff and security, drilling into us to follow the (restrictive) covid rules. Fun-busted daily, we were still paying shit loads for it.

You read these students accounts of Student life in lockdown online, most obviously carefully written, hosted on Uni blogs offering lame advice. Lockdown suggestions stretched from learning a new language, brushing up on public speaking or reading a good book... and to attend all online lectures that have been specifically designed. You'd read headlines in the media about students behaving badly, getting busted for throwing basement raves, police battering down doors, being monitored by helicopters with infrared cameras, rounded up with dogs, and arrested like real criminals. Consequently ending up in court with a heavy fine, a criminal record and at a topic in Parliament. 'Four Students Fined 40K for Throwing House Party in Tier Two Zone.' Exaggerated stories sensationalised by the media, fed the anger of the general public against these students. Back lashes on social built up hate, people who hadn't been able to go out of their gardens, being locked down in flats, attend funerals, see isolated grannies in care-homes, missing gym classes and going to the pub. It went on and on. Students who behaved badly became the scapegoats, someone to hate and blame in these torrid times. The majority of us lived to lockdown rules (some of the time).

On campus, we realised it was different from the restricted lives of the general public and for students who lived off campus. There was a feeling that we had more freedom. A little compensation for us missing out on the normal student experience we'd expected. It was mostly second and third year students living off campus, viscerally commenting on social media about being mugged off paying Uni fees, being locked down. We began to appreciate that we, most probably, had more freedom on campus than anywhere else in society. There became an awakening that our student experience was going to be unique, like nothing ever experienced before at Uni, living through a modern day war without the threat of bombs and national conscription. We just had to make the most of our lockdown.

Within weeks, we had adjusted to campus lockdown rules, and our socialising had evolved into something that we enjoyed. Our bubbles were tight-knit but it seemed that the quieter students, less naturally outgoing, became included and unified in their bubbled social groups. Students who wouldn't have been seen at The Warehouse on a Wednesday night, began to have a laugh in their own bubbles. We were all in it together, bubbled but more unified.

Anyone handy with a pair of hair clippers became sought after, and bartered for alcohol. One lad with clippers, became known as the barbaric barber. There were plenty of bad hair cuts knocking about, hidden under baseball caps, after he'd been hacking, With gyms and sports clubs closed, we synchronised gym training on Strava, competing with reps of burpees, squats, push-ups, jumping lunges, inter-dispersed with sprints. This was all lockdown friendly and quickly evolved into a campus league. Even tutors joined. Other virtual group activities formed, and existing clubs and societies quickly adapted to this new online format.

NIghtlife wasn't as easy to fix though. It started with bubble parties that escalated into block parties, spiralling into full blown hall parties, all quickly shut down by security. Security was reassuring when it came to more serious incidents, but could spoil the fun. Patrols around halls became more frequent, students had ID taken, cameras recorded us, and students were disciplined and fined by hall managers. However, we discovered ways around it.

Students unpicked loops holes in campus lockdown rules, which were pretty vague and open for interpretation. Common rooms became clubland, kitted with decks and lasers. Provided we started early and didn't exceed the numbers in rooms at any given time, we were ok, with one drawback, no music after eleven. It was a start, and even security agreed that the rules were murky, and would move on.

Shot-runners in teams of around six, ran through each hall on campus, downing vodka laid on in sixteen common rooms. It was known as 'hall-hopping' but the flow always collapsed somewhere along the line, due to the amount of alcohol, speed of drinking, combined with the mad dashes in fresh air, between shots. Eventually, security would catch large drunken groups, raving in one room, turn the music off and disperse the hall-hoppers. Didn't really matter, we just ran to adjacent halls for another one. This escalated to serving up stronger drinks, with dangerous looking mixtures scooped from buckets. Not very covid safe. It was unknown if anyone completed a full run. Nobody remembered.

One Sunday, it was blowing a gale. Trees had fallen throughout the campus. It was pretty dangerous at times. Security vans whizzed about, roads were cordoned off, and tree surgeons were busy with chainsaws. We saw this from the roof of our hall. Puffa jackets on, headphones blasting wicked beats, arms outstretched. We were flying. It was wicked. In better weather, we used the roof as a look-out for security patrols. Just hang out there, with a few cans, sharing their whereabouts on WhatsApp. False noise complaints worked well as a diversion too. Fire alarms were commonly activated across campus, and often synchronised at varying times during the night, either by smashing the break-glass or spraying deodorant on sensors. Parties would continue outside until security shouted a false alarm.

It didn't all go our way. Three dumb-asses in our hall found it amusing to activate alarms five or six times a night. Beyond a joke. Vigilante students patrolled corridors in an attempt to catch them. And they did. They were later fined for covering a hall fire sensor with a condom, so they could smoke. We as students, were now making our own non-written rules. The extreme of this, some students converted to hall snitches. They became victimised by others, repeatedly banging on their doors on boozy nights. Hall managers and security were aware, without being caught red-handed or having camera evidence, there was nothing to report.

The Uni was rather lenient towards student behaviour, and had an empathy towards us on the whole. After being reported, nothing too serious happened, maybe an advisory notice or fine. Rarely did a student get thrown out of halls for raucousness. We were, both students and staff, in this unusual predicament together.

One hot Sunday, through social media we held the biggest illegal rave on the sports field with over a thousand students. At the time, the general public could only drink in pub gardens, with table service, four to a table, without music. Security and police monitored us but didn't attempt to stop the party. They were more occupied with the string of Uber drivers, delivering bags full of booze, Nandos, and other unknown substances.

We're now back to some normality, relaxed rules with social areas fully open, and lectures conducted in theatres. The covid test marquee continues to open, as a reminder that some variants are here to stay, probably longer than us. Student life rolls on, it's vodka shots in common rooms, and Tom Zenetti at The Warehouse.

HAIR'S BREADTH

The arrival of summer brought about the perfect opportunity for a barbecue in the garden. As we basked in the warm sun, sharing laughs and swigging cold beers, we realised our supply was running low. I volunteered to make the ten minute trek through the tree lined streets of Mapperley Park to the nearest Lidl store.

On my walk, I noticed a man sitting outside the store with his dog on a leash. He appeared to be homeless, but I pushed that aside and quickly entered the store to restock our drinks. However, as I left with two heavy bags, guilt crept in. While I was enjoying a carefree afternoon, this man seemed to be struggling at rock bottom.

Feeling compelled to do something, I handed him a four-pack of beer. A grateful smile lit up his face as he thanked me. Being drunk myself, I sat down next to him and struck up a conversation while making a fuss of his friendly Staffordshire Bull Terrier. As we talked, he shared bits and pieces of his life in no cohesive order, but later I managed to digest what he had told me, and understood his story. He was younger than I initially thought. Life had not been kind to him, living rough had taken its toll. He was up for a good chat and very eloquent. The more time I spent with him, the more I wondered how he ended up in this situation. What battles had he fought?

As we cracked open another can of beer, he told me that just a few years ago, his life was filled with love and happiness. He was happily married with two beautiful children, lived in a nice house, and had a good job, with all the comforts one could ask for. But then everything changed. His daughter went from being a vibrant teenage girl to withdrawn and moody, her grades dropped and she lost interest in things she once loved. Unknown to them, she was being bullied online.

One morning, the paramedics arrived at their door without warning. Someone must have alerted them. His heart sank as they rushed past him and up the stairs to try and save their daughter. But it was too late. Their world shattered in that one moment. Life as they knew it was over. In the midst of their unspeakable grief, they turned on each other, blaming themselves for not seeing the signs or doing more to protect their daughter. Despite having parental controls in place, she still managed to find ways around them and continued to search for information on how to end her life. How can these multi-billion dollar platforms allow a young girl to die?

As time passed, his wife couldn't bear the pain any longer and left, taking their youngest child with her. He was left alone with nothing but guilt and sorrow, turning to alcohol as a coping mechanism. Slowly but surely, he spiralled into darkness, losing everything he had worked hard for in just six months. The house was gone, the job was gone; all stability and hope were lost, cutting all strings with everyone he knew.

He found himself on the streets, with only his demons for company. Mental illness took hold, fueled by the tragic loss of his daughter and subsequent collapse of his life. In those moments of despair, all he wanted was to disappear into oblivion. The pain was unbearable; the light had gone out of his world forever.

He was born in Aston, Birmingham, a region known for Premier League football with Aston Villa and being the birthplace of heavy metal band Black Sabbath. However, this area also had one of the highest crime rates in all of Birmingham. He grew up in this chaotic world with his brother and sister by his side.

He elaborated further, explaining that living on the estate meant everyone knew your name. It was a cliché but it held true. When there was any kind of disturbance outside, people would peek through their curtains, and it was a guarantee that several curtains up and down the street would be twitching in unison.

Outsiders always had exaggerated tales to tell about the estate - maybe about a drug bust or a supposed stabbing that didn't make it to the news. Sometimes there was some truth to these stories. People always chatted at the bus stop, and when the bus arrived, there was always an awkward standoff as to who would get on first. If you needed anything, someone on the estate would know the right person to help you out - whether you needed a mechanic, handyman, or affordable plumber. Parking was a constant source of arguments; while no one owned a specific spot, if someone parked in the wrong space, your car would be keyed. Despite outsiders' perceptions of this area being littered with burnt out cars, it wasn't the reality - most of the time.

As we sat there, cracking open another pack of beer, he opened up even more. He explained how much could be revealed about a person's life just by looking at the front of their house - for example, closed curtains at number 22 indicated a death in the family, while a dirty front step at number 47 suggested that the resident enjoyed meddling in others' affairs more than maintaining their own home. The type of car parked in a driveway and a Sky satellite dish, could also hint at someone's financial status, and upgrades like double glazing, signalled whether the house was still owned by the council or by its occupant. One man on the estate always kept his grass verge immaculate, even though it wasn't his responsibility - just an example of normal life on the estate.

With a shake of his head and one last swig from his can, he then told me about his older brother Charlie who had moved to Handsworth, another tough neighbourhood. His sister Amber lived in a pretty village in Staffordshire, but he hadn't seen her in a while. He stopped for a moment, composing himself before opening another can... and then continued.

His brother Charlie, simply known as The Muscle, was involved with drug dealers and their dangerous practice of county lines, transporting drugs across different areas and boundaries, often using vulnerable children who have been excluded from school or were in care. These kids were promised easy money and respect, but instead were threatened and manipulated by Charlie's gang. This menacing lifestyle was portrayed as glamorous through music videos, social media posts, and street talk. Snapchat became a popular tool for recruitment and showing off wealth, making it easier for the gang to target vulnerable youth seeking status and acceptance. Idolised by younger kids on the estate, he appeared to live a lavish life with expensive cars, flashy jewellery, and apparent wealth. But in reality, it was all a front.

Eventually, Charlie gave it all up, and left his criminal past behind. Last he'd heard, Charlie was in a suit selling high-end cars at Arnold Clark.

Despite his difficult situation, he remained composed and charming as he told his fragmented life story. On my walk back home, I was lost in contemplation. His story had me reflecting on my own life and relationships, and it made me realise how easily I could stumble into darkness. When I finally arrived at home, I didn't have any bags of beer and wine with me. He needed them more than I did, at least for the time being.

NOT FORGOTTEN

Hello mum. You alright. What you been up to?
Oh. Hello. It's you. Yes. Yes. Usual things.
It's roasting in here. Have you been out? It's sunny out there. Come on grab my arm, we'll go and sit in the garden for a change. See I told you it was sunny.
Yes. It's lovely.
Alfie played football this morning. Scored two and they won. I was ref again.
Oh yes. That's nice.
They're serving tea. Fancy a cuppa? I'll wave her across.
Yes. Yes. That would be lovely.
Think Ruth's coming up next week.
Ruth?
Yes Ruth. My sister. Your daughter.
I know Ruth.
Do you remember my name mum? It's Robert.
There's a breeze Robert. Can we go inside?

Hello mum. Brought you these chocolates.
Oh. Hello. Oh yes. I like those.
Do your friends want some? I'll hand a few out.
Mmmmmm. That's lovely.
Remember when you took your class to the zoo. What happened?
Zoo. Yes. The zoo. Ate his coat.
Who did mum? Who ate his coat?
Elephant. The elephant ate the little boy's coat.
And then you had to deal with his angry poor mother when the coach dropped the kids off.

Hello. It's Sunday mum. Have you been to church this morning?

Yes. Yes, I think so.

We used to go to church and Sunday school every week didn't we. Apart from dad. He went golfing. Then what did we do mum? What did we do every Sunday?

Yes. Every Sunday.

Who did we go and see every Sunday mum?

We went to Auntie Lila's. And Grandma's.

See you can remember. Auntie Lila used to give me and Ruth chocolate. And we weren't allowed to play in the garden. Uncle Osmond would bang on his bedroom window if we trod on his plants. A retired headmaster who hated kids. Every week. Same routine. Sometimes I could bring a friend. You let us walk from Auntie Lila's to meet you at Grandma's. We went over the pit slag-heap as a shortcut. Up to our knees sinking in muck.

Great Houghton. Yes.

When we got to Grandma's you told us about the school in Wales. The one that got buried by the sliding slag-heap. Aberfan. Never forgot that.

Yes. The school.

Hello mum. What are you eating?

Eating?

What are you chewing? Let's have a look. It's meat. When did you have dinner? Spit it out. Why haven't you got your teeth in? Excuse me. Has she lost her teeth?

What you doing in bed mum. Resting?

Oh. Hello.

It's Robert mum. You tired?

Yes.

I'll open your window. It's too hot in here. No wonder you're tired.

Yes.

Just thinking the other day about our holidays. Remember Fleetwood. Mount Hotel. We went there a few times, didn't we. There was that old waitress. Emma. Remember her. Wasn't that the place I got lost. You couldn't find me. Think I must have been a couple of months old. Dad came back into the hotel room with Ruth and you said I'd gone.

Yes.

I'd rolled underneath the bed. You couldn't find me could you.

Yes. No.

And that time you left me outside the butchers in the big pram. You and Ruth went off without me. Think you'd forgotten you had a baby! Was the Scotty dog tied to the pram too? I can't remember the details. We'll ask Ruth. She might remember. When I was about three, that fish monger lifted me up in the market and shouted "Who's lost a little lad?" I actually remember that happening. He stunk of fish. It was a big fish market then. Didn't we see a whale there?

Yes. Fish shop.

That's right. Your mum ran the village fish shop didn't she. You told me about that tramp your mum gave chips to everynight. That was a nice thing. What's his name. Old Bacon Joer. Remember him mum. And your dad, he was the village undertaker. Horse drawn carriage. Think we have his top-hat somewhere. They used to say 'build 'em and bury 'em.' Suppose you did.

Yes.

Auntie Mabel took the fish shop after Grandma. Then cousin Alison. I've not been to Great Houghton for a long time. Saw Alison at the football match. I took you to the match once. Barnsley versus West Ham.

Yes. I like ham.

Hello mum. It's me Robert. You know Alfie and Daisy don't you.

Oh yes. David.

It's Daisy mum. Not David. And Afie. My two kids. Your grandchildren.

Yes. Yes.

Pass her those chocolates before you eat them all. My mum looked after you both when you were born. Stayed in our flat in London for weeks helping Jess deal with you Alfie. I had to go back to work and she stayed for weeks. Helped your mum out. And you Daisy. When you were born I had to fly to Cape Town with work. Think you were three days old. My mum got on the coach from Barnsley. Remember that mum. Looking after these two, when they were babies?

Yes. Yes. They were babies. I sang to them.

You took Alfie in the pushchair for a walk and got lost, didn't you mum.

Hello mum. Why are you eating here on your own?

Oh. Am I?

Sunday Roast. Is it good? You been to church this morning mum?

Yes. Church.

Remember Chi-Chi mum. That kitten followed you and Ruth home from school. We took her in and looked after her. Dad put butter on her paws so she wouldn't run away. We had her for sixteen years. Fluffy tabby. We've got a black and white cat now, from a rescue centre. Harry. Very intelligent cat. Jess loves him. You had a dog when you were little didn't you. During war time. Bob. A black labrador sent up from Sandringham. One of the Queen's gun dogs. You told me the story about it, catching the bus in the village to meet your dad at the pit. The bus driver got to know the dog. He'd drop Bob off at the pit to meet your dad. Clever dog. Remember Tim the Black and Tan dog, mum. You and Ruth bought it at the pet shop and met me after school. Alsatian crossed with a beagle. He was a good dog. Apart from when he chewed the neighbour's tortoise. That was bad. When I'd gone away to school, dad used to take him to the club. And when dad died, Tim went on his own. They'd give him crisps and half a beer in his own bowl. Well, a Jonnie Walker ashtray. Have you finished your dinner? Come on, let's walk you through to the main room. They're playing old songs. Here there's two comfy chairs.

Thirsty. Cup of tea.

Right, I'll get you one. Wash that dinner down. Vera Lynn. You know this one. You were smuggling pork in your saddlebag when this came out. Your dad used to kill a pig illegally and you'd innocently take cuts, wrapped in brown paper on your bike, to people in the village. When you didn't want to go to school you'd forget your gas mask on purpose. They'd send you home.

We'll meet again, don't know where, don't know when...

Happy birthday mum. It's Robert. Jess and the kids are here. Got you some presents. You've had lots of cards. And there's some unopened presents. Here you go. Help her open it. That one's from Ruth mum.

Isn't that lovely. Feels beautiful.

It's a jumper. Here, we've a cake. No candles. It'll set the fire alarm off. Can't have that can we mum. Reminds me. My dad's 80th, all the oldies were all sitting in the garden when I turned up. All been on the sherry. Never seen them drunk before. There were some stories. Reminds me that you were all young once. Happy birthday mum. Open that window. It's boiling in here.
Mmmmm. NIce cake.

Hello mum. You awake? No. I'll put your radio on. You like Radio three. See you next week.

Hello mum. It's me. Your son, Robert. I'll pull up a chair next to you. Got our photos on your wall. Those gold frames. Makes us look like royalty. I was eight. What can I remember when I was eight. Oh yes. We all set off to Auntie Lila's and there was that smell. We all thought it was dad. Turns out he'd trodden in dog dirt. All over the clutch. We had to go back home and you washed it off. First time we'd ever been late visiting. You were still teaching when I was eight. I was a herald in the puff parade. Remember that Sunday School parade. All the churches marched under their banners through town. Ruth was Sunday school queen. Queen Marigold. She's coming to see you next week.

Hello mum. Ruth's here. I'm not stopping long but Ruth's here all day. Open that window. Too hot. It's always too hot. No wonder she's sleeping all the time. I would be. Radiators are on full blast. You can't turn them down. She's still got her birthday cards up. Put them in her drawer. Here, there's another one from auntie Betty. See you later.

Hello mum. It's Robert. What you been up to. Have you been teaching all week. Been to church. Are we going to auntie Lila's, Grandma's, then auntie Madge and Mabel's later? I can make a hot coal fire. Grandma taught me. It's all about layers and enough air getting through. It's pea-picking time. I'll be going with Auntie Madge. Spend all day in the fields to earn five shillings a day. Taught me the value of money she did. We used to visit Auntie Lenna's as well. I can only just remember that. You liked Lewis didn't you mum. I remember his photo in his army uniform. Didn't auntie Lenna's little girl get killed by an ice-cream van before the war? Grandma sent you to live with her.

Hello mum. It's Robert. We've been on holiday. Got you some chocolate and a postcard. I'll leave them on your table. It's hot in Turkey. Too hot for you. You didn't like the heat do you, but dad did. He'd be out in the garden burning his forehead, sitting on the bench by the apple tree. I planted that from seed. That apple tree. Got chopped down. Remember the cat had whisked the goldfish out of its bowl. Dad scooped up the dead fish up with the calendar from the wall, and through it on the rose-bed. It was there all day, until I noticed it was alive. Lived on for years. Holidays. We were always going away. Dad would hitch the caravan and we'd be off. A rainy week in a field. I threw and smashed a bottle on a dry stone wall. You saw me do it through the caravan window and slapped my legs. Think of all the animals that could get hurt, you said. You were right. Or was that your teacher-skills. I just shouldn't smash bottles. One thing that was a constant going away, apart from the rain, was the pub. There was always a pub nearby. We'd drink cider and Cherry-B playing cards in the caravan. Dad would be in the pub, chatting away with whoever was at the bar. Thinking about it. You never went to the pub. Only for a lunchtime meal. On Sundays, my lunchtime job was to pour liqueurs for us all. I was seven.

Hello mum. Let's open that window. That's better. No wonder you need a rest. You spent your whole life looking after everyone else, but never really looked after yourself. Falling down the cellar steps hurt you. Even when you went out in the evening, it was always for a good cause. I suppose that was your reward. You looked after my dad when he had a stroke in Belgium on holiday. You got him back home, delirious and ill. But you did it. I was only bothered about smuggling that flick-knife home hidden in Ruth's bag. You worked out that it was better for me that I went away to school. Spent the money inherited from grandma sending me to a boarding school, 'to get away from it all.' Maybe I was doing your head in getting in trouble whilst you were caring for dad. It was the best thing you ever did for me. Sending me away. To go there opened my eyes. Changed my life.

Hello Mum. Me again. Thought I'd say thanks for the 5K you lent me fifteen years ago for the deposit to buy my flat in Islington. Never did pay you back. And for sticking up for me when I'd been throwing blackberries at Fanny Husband's garage. It was me not Ann, but you believe my lie. Bangers, baked potatoes and beans were always a winner for my birthday parties. I set off the box of fireworks in the garage. Choking. We could have died. Your grandson Andrew didn't throw Christmas pudding at you. It was me. You were given valium to calm you down after you'd found me drunk, naked on the roof singing and throwing up. Another. It was my 30th birthday. You baby-sat my mate's baby at Butlins in Minehead for a weekend. We were out partying. Drinking. Sniffing coke. That fifty quid you gave me to take Cathy, my Canadian cousin out for a night out in Sheffield. We got on too well. Those cow bells above the hall door gave us away in the early hours. Sorry you caught us at it.

Hello   mum.   It's   Robert.   Your   son...
It's   ok.   You   don't   have   to   remember   anything.

I'll remember for you.

THE BARISTA'S EAR

Saturday 18th February 5.00am, crickets sound from my iphone alarm, a hint that Summer does actually exist even though it's hard to believe this early in the year. I was rudely awoken by the wind gushing at my ill fitted window that rattled all night. 'Wooden frames look traditional' I firmly believed, but uPVC has more benefits, especially in those harsh Winter months, so the leaflet pushed through my letterbox claimed. Well wrapped for the bitter cold, I was up and out driving within ten minutes, a routine beginning to be well rehearsed. Ritually opening up the lock-up, situated on a small industrial estate on the edge of town, lit by a temperamental motion floodlight. Electrician I'm not, but I thanked my fingerless gloves handling the metal bolts and shutters. Hitching on the mobile coffee tricycle, I was on my way to the Market Square.

By 05.45am, the Square was brought to life by bustling local marketeers preparing their stalls. It was a synchronised team event, dropping off goods from vans, trollies whizzing to and fro. "Is that coffee machine on mate?" The mobile coffee tricycle is the newest addition to the Square. Many stallholders are third generation, and often say it's a dying market due to retail parks and the lack of car parking in the town centre. "This market was triple the size, crowded with hundreds of folk all day. Talk about gossip! It all happened here." There's an underlying sense of nostalgia.

Drawing people away from the likes of Starbucks and Costa "is good for our trade too." The mobile coffee tricycle business had aspirations to become a shining hidden gem in an old traditional market place. In these cold Winter months, people were sporadically venturing into the Square to experience the historic market, with fruitiers, butchers, greengrocers, cheesemongers, fishmongers, cobblers, army surplus extraverts, bric-a-brac-ers, florists, and ready-to eat street food, a real living culture. And now my specialist coffee tricycle. From behind the steaming Fraccino coffee machine, I began to remember faces and their choice of drink. Knowing a customers' order, added a personalised friendly touch, combined with some knowledge of the coffee world. Offering specialist barista recipes that the High Street chains don't, went a long way to build up the count of regulars. Describing the difference or similarities between a latte, flat white or cappuccino, offering a ristretto to try instead of the more common espresso… always with enthusiasm, became a differentiator. Regulars stayed to chat, and began to open up, sharing snippets of their lives.

06.40am:
The Duty Solicitor. Americano (cold brew in Summer)
"Why do I do this job! All-nighter again. Teenage kid, e-scooter drug courier. Gave the police the runaround. Got landscapers in at seven. Wife's changed her mind. New layout this time. Cost me 20K already. 'Wider entertainment areas,' she says. Her big 40th in June. Flying in the family.
Costing me another fortune. Doesn't like her new C-Class. Says it's for Uber drivers, 8K loss driving off the forecourt. Nightmare! Why do I do this job? You can guess why. Another americano. Thank you."

07.40am:

The FishMonger. Black with a dash of milk.

"See Sainsbury's and those yuppy flats over there… it was full of market stalls. They queued getting off buses. Market was one way then, heaves of people five deep in a continuous snake. Must have been half a dozen fish stalls then. People ate more fish. Don't know how to cook it nowadays, unless it's breaded or in batter, frozen from a supermarket ready for the oven. Dying trade I tell you. Sixty years I've been here. I was eleven when I started here with my dad, bless him. I'm still going home stinking of fish though. First customer won't be here for half an hour. She buys fillets for her cats. Some days are not worth my while opening up to be honest. Not these days. Gets me out of bed though."

10.15am:

The Boxer. Double espresso.

"Thanks mate. A pick me up. Just come off a night shift at Sainsbury's. Five hours of high intensity training today. Mix of mitt work and sparring, running, strength and boxing drills. Killer. It's been hard. These sessions hurt. Weight nearly there though. Gotta keep going. Got the fight in two weeks. Olympic team qualifier. Fifteen years, and now it's my big chance of making it. Getting in the team helps, but you have to go on and medal to make decent cash. Can't keep on relying on family support. The time commitment, the sore muscles, strict diet, the bad headaches, no social life… none of that is as hard as living off those handouts. So it's the big one! A must win. Or I could throw it in the second for 5k. lol."

11.35pm:
Mediterranean street food chef. Cortado.
"Broke down Tuesday morning again. "Fuel pipe. Could have gone up in flames!" he said. Doubt that. It was pissing down! "Got to keep an eye on these 50's Citroën H vans. Looks smashing though!" he said. Held my brolly over him, head under the flipped bonnet, then gave him a waffle. Funny. Best thing we ever did was buy that van. Customers love it- expect me to pop my head out the hatch speaking French though! Come by before you hitch out love, I'll give you something to take home. Say the sun's coming out this afters. Ta-ra mon bon ami."

13.10pm:
No fixed abode. Mocha extra chocolate and popcorn (free)
"Yeah I'm ok, suppose. In a hostel now. This morning, I had me money nicked, didn't I, left me handbag hung up when I was in the shower. Thieving bastards. I'll kick 'em in if I find out who. F*cking smack heads aren't they. Only had 25 quid 'til Thursday. Hostel staff are ok. Helping me out. Think I'll stay there for a bit. Better than renting a room for a f*ck. Thanks for the drink mate."

15.35am:
Labradoodle owner. Flat white.
"Hi…like my outfit. All glammed up and somewhere to go! Meeting the boys here… then cocktails in Bar Freedom, a bite in Halfway to Heaven before hitting The Karaoke Hole. Hey, they're getting out of that Uber. Just today, please can you make us five espresso martinis. Here, I've got Vodka and Kahlua, and… crushed ice. Boys! Told you he'd make them. Make it six, you have one with us! Jemaine's a

designer in London. Works for an agency that did those crop circles near Stonehenge…"

OPEN WINDOW

It happened in the 90's when we lived in Covent Garden. A tenement building opposite Royal Opera House, by the ballerina sculpture on Broad Street. It's a small link between Bow Street and Drury Lane. A great place to live, always bustling with tourists, with everything on your doorstep and five minutes walk from Soho. The three tenement buildings were Victorian built, originally for the poor who would have worked no doubt in Covent Garden flower market. How times have changed. The flower market, now reallocated to Wandsworth. Thatcher's 'right to buy' act of the 1980's allowed tenants of local authorities to buy their homes up to half the value. You would have to have been mad not to have bought, especially in WC2. We were renting from someone who had luckily bought the property at a steal ten years earlier, now renting it out earning a fortune. Who lives in Covent Garden though? It was the right place at the right time of our lives. The three of us, my best mate Tom and my girlfriend Jen, all in our mid-twenties with good jobs, living in the pupil of the eye of London.

The tenement building had a gaited communal courtyard with a tall wrought-iron gate, stairs left and right led to three stories of flats. Ours was at the end of a thin balcony walkway, beyond half a dozen neighbours' doors on the second floor. Every night a drunk would cut through from Drury Lane down Broad Street and piss on our outer wall. It was dimly lit by a Victorian street light, now using a low wattage bulb resembling candlelight. We would laugh at them from our window above. To be honest I've had a piss down there, staggering back to our flat. It's our wall.

In Summer the flat is boiling and you have to sleep with all windows open to the consequence of being able to hear surrounding night-time activities. Cabs picking up the hoity-toity after the finale of a ballet performance at Royal Opera House, contrasting with droves of clubbers on their way to hidden underground venues. It was Covent Garden after all. And we lived there. Around this time, a Uni mate asked Jen and I to star in an advert he was shooting for Evening Standard. We had to walk out of Conran's Bibendum restaurant in Chelsea, hand in hand then run across the road and kiss before going out of frame. It was dark. The roads had been hosed for added reflections. After half a dozen takes the film crew packed up, moved on to another London setting and we were paid fifty quid each for our effort. Only the other day, out of the blue, my friend was flicking through old files and discovered stills from the shoot, dated 1994. We looked so young and actually in love, then.

One thing you didn't need living so centrally was a car. Nobody had one. Not just the lack of parking spaces or unaffordable underground parking, but it was actually faster to walk. However, Tom had his childhood favourite model, a red Fiat X19. Now for a big lad, he looked more like Noddy than a hipster. His favourite parking spot was on Drury Lane. You can imagine how busy that road is every day. On occasions, he'd park streets away to his annoyance. One week the council placed notices on every vehicle stating that they needed to move for 24 hours for new tarmac to be laid. Simple instruction that Tom chose to 'ignore' as the council phrased. Countless phone calls with the council, regarding his car being towed away and put in their compound for illegally parked cars. A place that he was becoming more familiar with. The compound hadn't a record of the X19, Tom started to believe that his pride and joy had been stolen. Weeks went by, we were out in Soho in a basement club, made famous by young hip celebrities who enjoyed the odd line of coke. Famous personalities, who would normally be seen outside Mayfair clubs swarmed by paparazzi. This club was secluded and tucked away, not on the paparazzi map. It was our favourite haunt and we'd been members for a few years, (until it got raided and closed on the spot by the Metropolitan Police). It was a ten minute walk home from the club via Soho Square. Staggering through the square at three in the morning, there it was in all of its glory- the red Fiat X19. Now the small print in the legal stated that if your car is parked legally but in an area that was being resurfaced, then it could be removed and placed in the nearest free parking bay. This happened to be thirteen streets away. Needle in a haystack comes to mind. Didn't get a ticket though. Tom drove home, and we queued for the best club sandwich from an all-nighter cafe on Old Compton Street. Still beat him home.

Summer in Covent Garden and Soho was the best place on earth. Apart from maybe Venice, St Tropez or New York, pending on your style. That Summer felt like most of the world was visiting London WC2, sun shining, packed with tourists eating icecreams transfixed by street performers, pedestrianised areas full of tables with winding queues waiting for seats. Unless you knew better, it could be an exhausting day. It's Saturday and I'd been told we're invited to a garden party in Notting Hill, at the home of Jen's new boss. Whilst Jen was book shopping, I had a few lazy cocktails with friends, sat on the balcony in West Piazza, returning to the flat on time, only to be told that I was drunk. This party was important to Jen. Fiona, her new boss, had a tight social network that was apparently a privilege to be amongst. Jen needed a quick drink to put her in the mood, it felt more like a work event and she was nervous. In the bar, our conversation was one sided, aimed directly at me.

Let me explain. During the week we had gone to see an up and coming British jazz-rap band, Us3, at Club 101. I'd had a hard day and was well up for a night out. By the time we'd past security and were in the packed venue I'd sunk half a bottle of vodka. The place was buzzing and so was my head. After going to the bar, Jen had disappeared. The venue was on three floors with balconies, each as rammed as the next. Jen was nowhere to be seen. Sometimes, when under the influence of alcohol you can make poor decisions. At the time, I reckoned that I was making absolutely the right decision. Not just that. It was brilliant. Squeezing through the eager crowd awaiting the band, I worked my way to the front. I was the only one looking backwards from the stage into the crowd, searching for Jen with my somewhat blurred vision. That didn't work. The band hit the stage and the place erupted. I started jumping with the beats, pointing at my head as if to say, 'I'm here! Look! I'm here!' This went on for a few tracks and even the band were looking confused. Jen hadn't seen me. I resigned to the back and got another drink. After the band's second encore. Jen appeared, having ignored me and my effort, with a tutting kind of expression. The next day at work she overheard someone talking about this odd bloke jumping up, pointing at his head at a gig the previous night. Jen didn't let on who that drunken idiot was.

So the one-sided conversation was accepted like a naughty dog, ears back with sorrowful eyes. My eyes weren't that sorrowful, more like glazed with alcohol as I tried to follow the underground map. Minutes on the tube and we were at Notting Hill, with over blown house prices ever since the film. What I remember about the garden party is rather vague, but clear in parts. We must have been there for a few hours, my memory tells me ten minutes. Clear bits: big Edwardian house, pathway to the rear garden avoids guests using the grand front door, entering the house. Garden, grapevine on the back wall, gravel garden with terracotta pots with herbs. A punch bowl full of bubbles, mint leaves and ice, and a tray of glasses. Summer wear, women in pleasant floral dresses, blokes in white jeans or chinos and polished brogues, chatting in tidy groups. I'd already met the host, Jen's boss, through her younger sister who knocked around with some of my mates, frequently going with us to the club in Soho. Jen's boss, Patricia, a powerful character who loved a laugh was fluttering from group to group socialising as a host does. Jen was anticipating Patricia's next move to our small group. Well, not a small group. To us. The two of us. Jen's face lit up as Patricia said, 'Hi Jen. So good you could make it.' What happened next has never been forgotten.

I've tried to work out why this happened in the way it did. And the steps towards it. Having met Patricia before, and having had a laugh with her, I'd established in my head that she was up for a laugh. In Jen's head it was her new boss and owner of the company she worked for. To me, Patricia was the older sister of wild Olivia, who loved snorting lines of coke off bog seats in our Soho club.

What happened next, as Jen was talking to Patricia, I laid flat on the gravel and was looking up Patricia's floral summer dress from her woven white sandals all the way up her tanned legs, and in a Vic Reeves type of voice said, "Patricia. Sit on my face." From my recollection, it was funny and it went down well, so to speak. Patricia screamed with laughter. That caused others to look across, more laughter. At this point I hadn't considered one big thing. Jen. She was dying with embarrassment.

As we climbed the escalators at Covent Garden on our return, I stumbled, my foot catching the strap of Jen's shoe. It snapped in two, she turned and hit me full fisted in the eye then walked off in the direction of our flat. A couple of minutes later I entered the flat ready to apologise. A barrage of 'why we shouldn't be together anymore' hit me in the other eye. There was no coming back from this one. I was sitting on the window sill, not saying much at all. Tom heard the commotion and popped his head in the living room and quickly returned to his room as Jen continued her onslaught. Split second decision, I fell backwards through the open window.

It felt like slow motion. Half way through I decided it was a bad idea to leave the room that way and gripped the side of the window-frame with my legs. Jen attempted to pull me back and called Tom to help. Too late. I'd disappeared through the window and was lying on my back in the courtyard. Both ran along the balcony, down the stairs, kneeling beside me. Eyes still closed, I gave out a Beavis and Butt-head laugh, "Huh-Huh. HUH! HUH!" Tom had to stop Jen from kicking me in the ribs. The next morning, I sported a black eye and a few bruises on my side, bearing no marks from the fall. On our doorstep, just delivered, lay a bouquet of flowers. I handed them to Jen which made some head-way to resolving things.

A few weeks later, entering a pub on Charlotte Street to meet Jen and her old boss, I'd forgotten to tell her that it was this previous boss, a Kiwi woman, who had sent Jen those flowers that morning. I was greeted by the biggest slap in the face. Jen applauded.

DAISY'S PETS

HARRY

Today's the day. That's what I always tell myself when I wake up. The day that I'll be able to walk freely in my beautiful garden again, making the birds chatter as I stealthily crawl through the long grass. Today, I'll be their friend. I've missed those flappy things. Today's the day old wrinkly lady will call my name, offer me tuna on my favourite china saucer. Today's the day I'll rub my back lovingly against old wrinkly lady's legs. My heart sinks, as it's never the day. The lights go out in the evening, and I'm left on my old blanket in this tall caged box. Just like all the others who are also living in hope. I can remember my old wrinkly lady so clearly. Most of the others can't remember their owners because they were too young when they came here. Unlike me. They just want to play with their siblings again. I can hardly remember mine.

Today's another day but unlike yesterday Wellington boot girl has already swept out and cleaned the long row of tall caged boxes. It happens occasionally before more unfamiliar people peer at me. "Harry, aged nine years. Friendly and intelligent. One lady owner," they often said looking at the door, before moving on to other doors. I'd watch the unfamiliars come and go. I'm still waiting for old wrinkly lady to call my name once more.

"Harry aged nine years old," said a long haired girl. "Harry. Hello Harry." I heard another older voice, "Hello Harry! He's nine you know. Come on, let's look at the other one's again." But long haired girl didn't follow. "Harry. You look very friendly. I like you!" she said in a warm voice. I moved off my blanket closer to long haired girl's fingers that were poking through. The smell of cigarettes reminded me of old wrinkly lady, so I rubbed my back on them like I knew how to. I felt happy.

Wellington boot girl entered my cage smiling, then expertly whisked me into her arms. "Harry's a very intelligent cat. He lived with his previous owner all his life- until she died. He's been with us ever since. Such a character aren't you Harry. We'll miss you!". I wasn't sure what was happening. Was I going back to old wrinkly lady? I was carefully placed into a plastic box with my blanket. I peeked through a gated window. There was a clunk and chugging noise. I could see long haired girl sitting next to me and trees passing quickly. "You're coming home with us Harry. Your new home!" What did that mean? I felt scared.

The chugging stopped. I went to the back of the box, it wobbled as it was picked up. I didn't want to look out. A big male face appeared. "Hello! So you're Harry!" the face said abruptly. "Don't scare him! Go away Alfie," long haired girl shouted in a loud whisper. The box door opened. I could see a long wooden floor and large sofa rather   like   my   old   one.
Box or sofa. Box or sofa. Box or... I ran, skidded on the floor and hid behind the sofa. It felt safer. I hid in a ball. Eyes peered at me from above. "It's ok Harry. This is your new home," long haired girl assured. Legs and feet came towards me and a china saucer was placed on the wooden floor. "There you go Harry. Have some milk," the tall lady said. I didn't move. Long haired girl watched me in silence. Eventually, I thought I'd try the milk and stop being a

scaredy-cat. It tasted good. Welcome to a new home. It wasn't long before I felt at home. Long haired girl played with me and tall lady fed me very delicious food. Tall boy Alfie spent most of his time shouting at this rectangular box thing with black things over his ears. There was also old grumpy man. He would leave early in the morning, disturbing me, and come back at night, disturbing me again. Eventually, I got to know his daily routine.

After a few weeks I ventured outside. There were fluttering birds, trees, hedges, and a long stretch of grass with a shed at the bottom of the garden, rather like the one old wrinkly lady had. There were times in the house when I could hear shouting from tall lady, old grumpy man and long haired girl. I just hid behind the sofa until it stopped. Often with angry words, ending in tears. Words like 'weed' and 'tattoos' were used. Long haired girl used to bang the wall with her fist. Or run away. That upset tall lady and old grumpy man. Tall men in dark uniforms came to the house. Sometimes tall boy Alfie and old grumpy man would cheer at the rectangular box. Occasionally everyone would sit together, make comments or argue about singing coming from the box. Old grumpy man would shout, 'It's starting!' and long haired girl would light candles and make the room smell like flowers. Old grumpy man would bring in bottles and cans of liquids. They all watched the box happily. I liked them together like this. It was family, my family.

Old grumpy man was grumpiest early in the morning. Same routine everyday. Goes into the little room that smells of clean clothes, then he makes it smell of poo. Out he'd come in tight shorts with a light on his head. He wouldn't let me go upstairs to see long haired girl. His feet would appear through the gap preventing me from whizzing past. "Oi you little f*cker. You're not going upstairs they're sleeping," he'd grunt. Drink of water and off he'd go out the back door into the dark, with a bright light shining from his head. He can't see in the dark. Always the same length of time before I'd hear him come back, drenched, face covered in splats of mud. He always forgot. "Oi... Harry don't go up..." Too late. Ha! Outsmarted him. Old grumpy man wasn't allowed to go upstairs with muddy shoes so he couldn't chase me.

We'd have this little battle most mornings and I always won. Sometimes I'd hide waiting for old grumpy man to leave the door open, sneak upstairs and jump on long haired girl. She'd be asleep, so I'd tap her face with my paw a few times to wake her, "Harry! I'm sleeping." Then I'd dig my claws and purr. If I felt peckish I'd go and tap tall lady's face. She'd get up and give me food. Never dared wake up tall boy Alfie. Old grumpy man would come upstairs, "F*cking Harry got up stairs again!" I felt sorry for old grumpy man. Often, he'd be up most of the night not being able to sleep, especially on a Sunday night. Grey faced, he'd get a bottle from the fridge and gulp it down. Then he'd fall asleep on the sofa for a couple of hours and wake up more grumpy.

On hot sunny days I'd spend my time lazing in the garden. Never alone. Birds in every tree, and with this huge black rabbit. I kept away from it because it was so big and clumsy. Clumsy rabbit never went into the hutch, but lived under the shed. But I'd jump into the hutch and watch clumsy rabbit from there. If clumsy rabbit wasn't chewing, it was bouncing about looking for more food. Whenever new flowers appeared, a clumsy rabbit ate them. Tall woman wasn't happy about that.

There were afternoons when we both made ourselves scarce. Tall boy Alfie would repeatedly kick this ball in the air, counting numbers. When the ball went in the bushes he'd retrieve it, then start counting again. It was best not to hide behind bushes. That ball could hurt. Sometimes tall woman would spread a blanket, and sit looking at books and scribble writing. Clumsy rabbit would sprawl close by. Couldn't understand why clumsy rabbit didn't ask for treats. I loved my treats and tall lady gave me them whenever I wanted them. Then I'd let her stroke and tickle me. Life became so relaxed and enjoyable. Eating and snoozing in various parts of the house and garden.

Once there was a dark night with loud noises coming from the house, people wearing glitter and hats, jumping around laughing. I hid like I did on my first day, and watched as more entered with bottles and cans. I was ok. I'd learnt to hide from old grumpy man when he drinks from bottles and cans. This time I had to hide from everyone. After a loud shout, everyone followed old grumpy man out the back door with another old man carrying a box. In the dark they planted things in the garden. People were quiet, then started counting. Boom! Something exploded from the ground. Boom! Again. Everyone cheered as sparks flew into the air, "Happy New Year!" Boom! Boom! I watched through the window- unlike clumsy rabbit. Clumsy rabbit was out in the garden terrified. Tall lady and long haired girls shouted 'Stop!' as they shone light beams on clumsy rabbit cowering behind a bush. Clumsy rabbit kicked as she was carried into the house. Boom! It started once more, and so did the cheering. Clumsy rabbit was taken upstairs by long haired girls, jumped free and hid underneath the bath. Long haired girls kept whispering 'Koko! Koko!' Old grumpy man started thumping the ceiling downstairs with a wooden tool shouting 'Koko! Come out wherever you are!' Clumsy rabbit froze for hours. I was in my usual hiding place. Safe behind the sofa.

Venturing in other gardens was fun. Venturing across the road was even more fun. Across the road, between the houses, over a fence to other large gardens and allotments. Didn't venture out there too much because there were dangers to avoid. Every so often was enough for me. Most of my time I'd be observing life from the garden table keeping watch on the goings on. More to the point, I'd be ready to butter up tall lady. She loved giving me food and I loved eating it. I'd hang around her legs until she gave in. Easy. I demanded my favourite food. Demanded, I really mean emotionally coaxed with my big wide eyes, floating tail, exaggerated buzzing purr and tapping paw. This tactic never worked on grumpy old man or tall boy Alfie. Tall boy just passed on my demands to tall lady. Grumpy old man just said 'You're too fat Harry' and smiled at me. That's a word I often heard these days. People would say 'Harry' and 'fat' together in the same sentence. What did fat mean? Did it mean I was charming? When tall lady heard 'fat' she would stroke me and say 'he's not fat'. So I liked hearing 'fat' when she was around. Fat was good. Fat was happy. There were other names I often heard: roly-poly, chubby-tubby, lard ass, chunky, piggy, need a diet, pudding, and walrus. Not sure what they all meant but they all had the same response from tall lady. She'd melt, then stroke and tickle me, 'Harry's a very intelligent cat. Don't call him names.'

Today's the day they stopped calling me names. In fact they stopped calling me anything. What was today? I'd been out strolling late afternoon and it had started to get dark. I could see tall woman feeding long haired girl and tall boy Alfie through the kitchen window from across the road. Old grumpy man came round the corner on his squeaky fold-up cycle, and went inside. Maybe I'll go home soon, just a little longer waiting for tall woman to be alone. It's always easier to get treats that way. I started my trot from across the road. I had seen the car but had plenty of time. Plenty of time to run across the road, to get nice treats. There was a loud bump. I heard tall lady scream, "I know it's him! I know it's him!" Old grumpy man opened the kitchen door and ran to the road. "Harry!" he called as he picked something up in his arms and carried it to the back garden. I could hear tall lady screaming hysterically like I've never heard before. What had happened? Why was she so upset? I wondered what to do. So I sneaked past old grumpy man who was carrying a heavy dustbin liner, through the garden gate and upstairs to see tall lady. She was lying down on the landing floor sobbing. I sat with her. Then pawed her face. She didn't react so I pawed again. It seemed to go through her. Tall boy Alfie tried to comfort her and then old grumpy man. I pawed her again on her face but nothing happened. So I sat with her. I sat with her all night as she lay in a ball sobbing her heart out. I heard her whisper, 'Harry! Oh Harry!' I didn't leave her. I snuggled next to her but I couldn't make her smile.

The next day various people came round to the house to see tall lady. They hugged her as she tried to hold back tears but streams ran down her cheeks. I just sat on the kitchen table watching. Nobody stroked or tickled me, nor did I coax tall lady for for food. In fact for as long as I can remember, I didn't feel hungry or want treats. It felt kind of weird but good. From that day onwards, 'Harry' was seldom mentioned. I stayed close to tall lady everyday ready for when she did. I'd sit with her on the sofa whilst she read books and tapped letters onto a screen. I was happy. Happy that tall lady spent so much time with me there every day. Eventually I stopped trying to grab her attention with my paw, because my paw thing had stopped working. But I was happy. I could go upstairs when I wanted and sleep on tall lady's bed with her, even when old grumpy man was there. I'd watch her get ready, following her downstairs to make coffee and then leave in her car. I'd wait for her to come back, ready to curl up next to her on the sofa again. It didn't feel the same, but for me it was bliss.

Life continued like this for some time. Then one day old grumpy man and long haired girl came through the kitchen door with a bear on a chain. I sat watching from the kitchen table as the bear entered and filled the room. "WTF! It's massive!," tall boy remarked. Tall lady just stared then said 'What have you brought home Daisy!' This tickled me.

THAI

Wasn't sure where we were going but we were travelling north from East London out into the sticks as they say. Standing on the back seat with my head between the front seats, I was interested to see where we were heading and had a clear view through the front window. My panting breath made the driver's ear and neck warm. The side window opened. Daisy, as I now know her, was being squashed by me on the back seat. She attempted to stroke me but my backside and fluffy legs were in her face. What with my curly tail and all, not the best sight to begin a new relationship. Apart from the sound of passing vehicles and the wind gusting through, there was silence. Daisy and the driver didn't speak. The journey reminded me of my first time travelling down from Lancaster after being separated from my mother and siblings when I was very young.

How I came to be in another vehicle on another long journey five years later was quite predictable. Imagine a young East End London couple living in a small flat on the seventh floor with a fascination for American Akitas, and babies they were about to bear. Five years living with my, let's say, auntie and the young couple who really did love Akitas. Of course it was so impractical living in this small space, in this bustling city of concrete, next to the runway of City Airport. Quite fun squeezing into the lift every day to walk along the Thames promenade, especially as I got older and bigger. When I say bigger, I became oversized for my age, then simply oversized. To say I was the runt of the litter doesn't add up to me being abnormally larger than what's considered normal. My auntie was smaller, probably average, but she made up for it because she actually barked. Not a thing we American Akitas are known for. On occasions maybe, but auntie barked at things you'd expect more vocal dogs to bark at. This barking became an issue in the small flat, so auntie was told off many times as she barked at banging doors and people shouting in corridors. I'd just watch her as she took the scolding and chuckled inside. Auntie would wink at me. So life for five years was East London with my auntie and a growing family.

I didn't mind the baby being held on my back playing bear rides, and later, a toddler tumbling over me and snuggling me like a teddy. It was our fun in the flat that made life amusing for us all. But as I got older I didn't like fingers being poked in my ears so I developed a noise that expressed my emotion. A noise which was three quarters short humming and a quarter nasal growl (without showing teeth). My new mono-tone was my way of saying, 'Give it a rest please.' Surprising how impactful it became.

The predictable thing about the situation was the blunt realisation that two American Akitas, a toddler in a pushchair, a pregnant young mother, a father who was working seven days a week to make ends meet, a small flat and even smaller lift, wasn't workable. Something had to give and knew it was probably going to involve me. But that was ok. Don't worry about the future, live each day as it comes.

Things did change. Grandma had cancer and went into hospital to die, so we all moved into her council house just down the road. The house had an upstairs that auntie and I weren't allowed to go and a patio backyard with a shed. To make things easier and to give the family space, I started to sleep outside at night. Every little helps as they say. I'd sleep next to the glass doors so I could see auntie looking at me through the window. Her breath misting the glass and her nose making marks. I'd lie on my back showing my chest, paws hanging in the air, pretending to be asleep snoring. It tickled auntie and became our thing. Every night, I'd roll about on my back, snoring louder and louder with one eye on her to see her smile. Even today, I catch myself half asleep, rolling on my back thinking of auntie smiling back at me. Another funny thing, auntie told me that if I turned around three times before lying down, it was good luck. I believed her. Sometimes I do it because it reminds me of her. Auntie wasn't really my auntie but an older American Akita that we once had a litter of pups.

The journey wasn't as long as I'd expected. I'd enjoyed taking in life outside East London through the window, particularly the green countryside and lack of concrete. Daisy led me out of the car, awkwardly clambering to the floor. I followed her into the cottage onto cold terracotta tiles. I thought I saw a black and white cat arch its back on the kitchen table but maybe it was my imagination.

Nice kitchen with a red leather chesterfield sofa and a huge steel fridge freezer. No doubt it was stacked with delicious food. People entered and stared at me. 'WTF! It's massive!,' a tall boy remarked. A lady just stared then said 'What have you brought home Daisy!' There was odd tension in the air. One I was accustomed to. It's something I'm used to when meeting new people, probably because of my breed and obviously my size. I understand. So as not to scare people I act calmly, no sudden movements and never any barking. The room felt crowded and eyes were peering at me, so I calmly and slowly walked around sniffing. Wherever I went people seemed to move out of the way. A nervous lady who looked similar to the other said, 'Just let him smell the house.' So I did. Interesting smells. You can understand so much just by sniffing - a depth of history and personality.

It was a welcoming beginning to my new home. There were so many new discoveries every day, that it felt like a holiday. Walks were exciting, fields, woods, churchyards, with plenty of good places to go for a poo. So much better than the concrete jungle. That was messy. Now I could poop on grass, leaves, mud and in fields, all of which was a more private affair. Soon I had my favourite places where I could time it perfectly to get there, do my wiggle-walk, poo and away we go. As I got to know the place, I started to decide on my own routes. Head down, legs digging into the ground I'd hold out being pulled in their direction until the 'walkie' gave in to my way - the right way. Even in the middle of the high street with cars waiting to pass on either side. Head down, I'd win.The more we walked the more we went the 'right way'. Sometimes I didn't want to go home so I'd hold out until we went further, sometimes doubling the time out on my walk to the dissatisfaction of the 'walkie' - normally Daisy or her mum 'Jess'. I say time, because I'd rather walk slowly taking in the tapestry of smells than walk quickly missing clues of identification. Slow was best. Now Jess was the lady of the house who made most of the rules, but she was the easiest to convert. We'd just walk my way as soon as the front door was closed. Sometimes I couldn't decide and really wanted Jess to have some input at least, mix it up a little. But with her it was always down to me. This way. My way. This way. Poo. This way. My way. Home. When there was an easterly wind there was this very distinctive sweet smell in the air. Sat there with my nose in the air for hours, had me racking my brain about what on earth it could be. I registered it as undefined. Then on one of our longer walks over fields, I discovered pigs. What funny creatures they are! They fascinated me. Never smelt anything like them. The combination of urine, excrement, straw and pig swill was exquisite. There was a problem. I fell in love with the smell of pigs. This wasn't actually the problem, it was the fact that once near the pig pens I couldn't and wouldn't move. Something was triggered in my brain paralysing my ability to move, transfixed with my nostrils and the dirty strong smell totally absorbing my brain. It became an addiction. No matter how they shouted at me, dragging my thick neck, I couldn't move. It was as if I was hypnotised. After about an hour I'd come out of my hypnotic state enough to move. Sometimes I'd wake up realising that I'd been left tied to the pig pen. I hadn't even realised. Even when the so-called master of the house fixed an electronic dog collar to me (now banned) it didn't make me walk. My back legs would stamp as it buzzed but it failed to make me move. Eventually, as weeks went by, I grew out of this deep love affair.

The walks with master Robbie were more like vigorous exercise than a stroll. Hardly could I get my nose to the ground before he was moving me on either verbally or pulling me sharply. It got me into a new frame of mind, a pacier lifestyle. Smelling as we walked, with quick thinking and smell logging. At weekends when he was around, we'd venture far and wide, some of which were abandoned footpaths of old. He'd pull me through brambles, across newly ploughed fields, through woods and across streams. Even though I resisted here and there, I'd get back home feeling like I earned my roast chicken thighs, homemade gravy and perfectly boiled rice (by the way the chicken fat gave me the runs). I'll quickly mention young master Alfie. When we did go for walks, which was seldom because he was mostly out playing football or on his playstation, he'd always choose the short dog chain with the red leather strap. It was so short and he was so tall, that when I bent down to poo, he'd have to bend down too. That said he hardly ever bent down to pick up a poo... especially after roast chicken thighs.

Now Daisy was a different kettle of fish. She loved having me around her rather than take me on a walk. Let me explain. Daisy doesn't really want to go on a dog walk. Daisy wants to have me tag along, to hang out with her and her mates. Daisy then was all about Daisy, I had to fit into her lifestyle, not the other way round. Seeing life from Daisy's point of view was, shall I say, precarious. Let me try to explain. Daisy lived life on the edge. She lived in a desirable village, next to a small town, where she hung out with her friends from various estates. She was also volatile because she was 'Daisy' , a teenage girl who didn't recognise boundaries, with a big self-built reputation. That's where I fitted in. An American Akita is no 'Labrador' or 'Cockapoo'. An American Akita is 'a bear- like, intimidating watch-dog as well as a powerful guard-dog.' I was chosen to be an extension of Daisy's brand. Proof of her own brand identity. What she went through to build the 'Daisy brand' was a huge effort and was very taxing on her. Not just the expected teenage social media banter but real personal brand building with incidents that endorsed it. Whilst hanging out with her friends in the park, they would go over stories, laughing hysterically sometimes to the point of tears. I'd just sit there pretending not to listen as they continued to smoke weed and tell more stories.

Gradually the number of times that Daisy would take me along to meet her friends was on the decrease. The time she spent out of the house increased to the point where she wasn't coming home, even at night. I could feel the anxiety at home and see the grey worry on faces. A fourteen year old girl smashed out of her head in some unknown council house with her mates, without a care in the world about what grief she was causing and what harmful situation she was getting involved in. Everyone would be out looking for her, including neighbours and the police. Driving around knocking on doors, searching various parks and other teenage hang-outs. Her social media traces would indicate her phone battery had obviously run out, with the sudden absence of drug fuelled group selfies being posted. I'd watch as worried faces came in and out of the house without any news and without Daisy.

On a couple of occasions master Robbie had to leave work early in London to bail her out of a police cell. This only added depth to the Daisy brand to the point that her bad reputation escalated beyond belief. Then there was the school expulsion. Moving from one school to another more suitable to Daisy's creative ability didn't work out due to smoking weed on her way in to school and her shoplifting at lunchtime.These Daisy stories fed gossipers in our village, built a bad-ass image within her peer group and caused more dark cloud to settle over our home. I'd keep out of the way and watch the goings on from afar. Sometimes on my dog walks Jess would be in tears, often after explaining the current Daisy situation to familiar faces she'd bumped into around the village. They were all ears, as usual, and there was no getting away. On brighter days I'd spend most of my time chilling in the garden. Pending on the strength of the sun I'd be hidden in the shade behind a hedge, or spread out dozing on the grass... for hours. Time you enjoy wasting isn't wasted time. It's time well spent. I had time to think and reflect deeply about things. Buckets of time. Time is the great healer and I felt that the dark cloud of Daisy would pass and the sun would shine brightly again one day. I recognised vast swings in Daisy's mood. Sometimes she was happy and having a laugh then other she'd be screaming in her room punching holes in the walls. What was going on to make her so over reactive? A teenager yes, but this was off the scale of normality. It worried me. It also worried me seeing the stress it was causing Jess. I suppose it was the combination of work and Daisy that finally made her go to the doctors. I didn't realise at first but recognised that she was taking the tablets methodically each day. They certainly had an effect. Hard to describe but when there was a Daisy drama she didn't react so emotionally and her response was much lighter, like an acceptance. The anti-depressants numbed Jess through troubled times as the dark cloud of Daisy engulfed our home.

Master Robbie coped with these situations in his own different ways. He's quite simple to understand. Every week he smashed himself up going to work, smashed himself up training for whatever sports event he was targeting, and he got totally smashed on booze. Sometimes he couldn't remember cycling back home from the railway station in the early hours of the morning. He was so drunk, only to get up a couple of hours later to go back to work on his fold-up bike. It seemed that the industry he was in, was a 'work hard and really play hard' culture. How he kept all three balanced was an art form. How he mentally kept going was astonishing. When he kept the three separate it worked, but during this Daisy period those times became seldom. The wheels started to wobble. He became more tired, his sports performance suffered and he struggled at work. It became upsetting to see him in this downward spiral. Often he'd come downstairs in the middle of the night down half a bottle of wine and a handful of tablets. He couldn't sleep. He was scared to go to bed. A cold fear that I could feel. It became a regular pattern that he couldn't break. Master Robbie had the fear of going to bed, whereas I used to have the fear of sleeping. Let me explain.

Back in East London, as a young pup, I used to spend time in the backyard. Four brick walls, concrete tiles and wooden playhouse. Doesn't sound much but it was my space. I'd hang out there all day playing. Auntie would watch through the window. One morning I was aware of a strong scent of an animal similar to a cat or dog but different somehow. Each day it was getting stronger so it became a scent for me to monitor and log. One morning I heard a shriek like a crying baby... Auntie could only watch as I fended off three foxes. The concrete was now covered in blood, not all mine. That was the last time any foxes came in our backyard- but I was left mentally scared. Auburn fur has a unique scent and every time I get a whiff it reminds me of that day. Unfortunately even with my chilled personality, I developed anger trends towards Irish Setters. On occasions Jess had to apologise profusely to owners of that breed because of my actions.

Life was good. Two walks a day. Never the same route - I made sure of that. Sometimes I'd go for a trip in the car. Loved hanging my head out the back window feeling the gusts of air in my nostrils. I could pick hundreds of scents that I had logged. On very hot days Jess would drive me to the springs to paddle and cool down. That was so refreshing. Now and again I'd go to the groomers to shed my layers of winter down. Groomers would always be shocked at the amount of fur that would come off, well I am an Akita. That would cool me down, and help cut down the number of fur balls rolling around the house gathering under the bookshelves and sofas.

Often we'd go to the pub garden to find the hedgehog. I got good at that and knew just how much to bite without hurting either of us. It became a game of hide and seek between friends. Another friendship was with the black rabbit that lived under the shed in our garden. After chasing it for a few weeks or so the rabbit realised I didn't have the speed of a whippet. As I chilled on the grass she would lie next to me. There was no need to move - she'd be off as I twitched. We'd sleep out at nights together, smelling and listening to the wildlife. Foxes never visited our garden. In the heat of the day I'd hide in the shade behind the buddleia bush by the wall of the house. The black rabbit was always nearby... until the old girl died. I missed her, and couldn't bring myself to sleep out ever again.

Alfie had done well and finally left for university. There was a huge emotional gap in the house. Occasionally his limited edition Suzuki Swift SZ-R would spin round the corner and proudly get out of his pride and joy with a basket of washing and his X-box. The reason I emphasised the model of his car was to lead on to the reason why he got it in the first place. It was a big thank you gift. Thank you for not killing yourself and your friend, in that other tin box of a car when you rolled it three times on a hidden bend, on a wet Hertfordshire country road at midnight. No one would have believed anyone would have come out of that wreckage alive. But they did. He certainly did and his reward was an extremely quick but safer sports hatchback with a high insurance bracket to match. Motherly love. Don't roll it again. And he didn't, but as Daisy was driving up to park her car behind Alfie's shining black SZ-R outside the cottage in her new white Ford Ka with a red lipped grille and L-plates, Alfie chuckled as he watched from the kitchen door. This had an immediate knock on effect. Bang! Bang! I saw Alfie's face drop into shock and eyes filled with tears. Daisy had ploughed into the back of his beloved car and in turn shunting forwards into the neighbours BMW. Alfie ran to his room.

A few weeks later, there was an atmosphere I'd never sensed before. Master Robbie wasn't commuting as early nor as often. Something was bubbling. Something big and I couldn't work it out. There was a mixture of excitement, and anxiety in the air, especially from Jess. Robbie spoke about the business in London being wound down and having to close down client accounts. The for sale sign stood proud outside the kitchen door. We were planning to move. Men came and took everything away in two tall lorries. It took five of them to lift my dog house over the garden gate. Made us all chuckle even Jess for a few seconds. Seeing the house bare was very unsettling. I went from room to room but didn't know where to settle. It wasn't home anymore but a stark empty shell. We were moving to a new home with new dog walks... and new discoveries.

I've never been one for climbing stairs given the option but our new home had stairs, stairs and more stairs. Even hidden stairs. For a few days it was like family hide and seek. I couldn't find people, there were so many rooms. It took me all my breath to find Daisy on the third floor. Once there, breathless, I would stay there for hours as she unpacked. Hoards of cardboard boxes obstructed every room seeping the scent of paraphernalia from the cottage. Every day there were new discoveries. My dog house was perfectly positioned by the kitchen door with a full view of the garden, surrounded by tall trees and huge aged townhouses. Watching crows and magpies became my new pastime in our garden as everyone else worked away inside the house.

Each day we would go on different walks, sniffing along towering tree lined Victorian streets overflowing with leaves, to forest pathways and river walks. Sometimes to the river for a picnic on the river bank watching the cows graze and boats glide passed. We discovered old collieries, nurtured into nature reserves only ten minutes away. I'd hang out the car window on the back seat, gusts of wind making my fur engulf the air and finally come to rest in every nook and cranny. I loved paddling in ponds, making the car smell like my dog house for days.

Often we'd have guests. They'd wander through the house for the first time checking out each room on every floor, just like I did. Master Robbie would give a little history of

Mapperley Park emphasising the grandeur houses and magnificent trees, the vast grade II listed allotments facing our home and always the proximity to the city centre. Daisy was simply 'loving it' and enjoying life on the top floor with her ensuite bathroom and mirrored wardrobe. Alfie revelled in the nightlife with his mates, coming back in all sorts of states. Jess would compare it to Ashwell and the life we had come from. Everyone who visited loved our new home and the future it held for us.

And there she stood on the kitchen floor. Daisy had shocked Jess and master Robbie once again and brought home a 10 week old 'Staffy' as master Robbie put it - which in turn Daisy claimed she was an 'American Bulldog / Bullmastiff' cross. It's 'not stopping or I'm leaving' were the repeated words from Jess. 'It' named 'Betsie' by Daisy (and in time 'Betty' by master Robbie) did stay, mostly in Daisy's room for the first few days. The young pup had that fresh smell about her which I couldn't get enough of. Lively little thing. She played rough, whilst I'd be careful not to stand on her.

The coming months were good days. Many old faces came to visit our new home and it was warming to see them again. I liked familiarity in our new environment. There were old faces I recognised and Alfie would bring back many faces old and new from University. It felt like home. I'd discovered new strategic places to chill so I could keep an eye on the comings and goings throughout the day and night. Drunken legs striding over me as I peered through half open eyes. Our new environment could host so much more for us all.

Chilled was not a description for Nowty Betty, quite the opposite. I'd grown to be aware of people and their behaviours but she was still in her infancy, barking at everything and play-nipping everyone who came in the home. It made me chuckle. Often I'd watch her chew away on belongings knowing full well that she'd be told off. The stair-carpet, shoes, plastic objects, whatever interested her. It didn't go down well and there were tears... the total destruction of her expensive glasses eventually broke Jess. There became a change in routine in the home. Instead of family being around most of the time, they were out at work like they used to be. It meant that I spent more fascinating time watching the antics of Nowty Betty. Often I'd tell her off if she turned her excessive energy nipping and play-fighting with me. Once was enough to make her stop. Jess was spending more time working when home, Daisy went out for short hours during the day, and master Robbie was away at odd stretches of time that baffled me. There was a different energy in the home.

Then along came Baby Lily. Daisy had eventually given birth to a beautiful girl. I love the smell of babies. It's been wonderful watching her develop each day and hearing her say her first words. Soon she'll be running around the place chasing Betty. Time flies. We've been on some beautiful walks together. Lovely being part of our family and now with Lily it's even better.

I tried to hide my discomfort, the way I was sliding myself downstairs on my back legs. They were on the way out. It happens to big dogs like me. Rest. I'd spend my time quietly on my own, drifting through my memories, reflecting on my wonderful life, all the kindness, and the ones who I deeply loved.

I went on my favourite walk in the woods yesterday. It was raining, so we didn't go the long route. I took in all the wonderful smells in the meadow grasses, rich soils and fallen leaves. For some reason, there was the smell of pigs in the air. Nowty Betty would run out of sight then come bouncing back, playfully nipping my backside as she raced past.

Now my time has come. I looked deeply into everyone's eyes saying goodbye. Master Robbie's tearful eyes looked back as Jess held me to the very end.

BETTY

Knock-knock! Something triggers in my head. Who's there! My hair stands on end. Time stops. Rush of adrenalin hits my brain. Involuntary urge. Can't stop it. I'm running on the spot, sliding on the Edwardian tiled floor, trying to sprint to the front door. Slow motion. My softer facial expression changes to fight-face. An ascending deep rolling growl comes from within me. Real speed. I fly at top speed towards the door. I skate at full pelt banging into the caged letter box. "Grrrrrrwwwwrrrrwww!" It's so primal. I'm buzzing. I'm at the door. I'm off my head. It's a person! Quick. Go to the window. "Grrrrrrwwwwrrrrwww!" Jump on the posh chair tipping it forward onto the window sill. Who the f*ck is it? They're still at the door. Jump. Run back to the door. It's a package. A person with an oversized package. Yodel. Boo Hoo. I don't care!

"Grrrrrwwwrrrrwww!" Back to the chair. They're moving! Back to the window. "Grrrrrwwwrrrrwww!" Woof! Woof! Woof! Woof! You Yodel Boo Hoo parcel man! Woof! Woof! You Yodel f*cker! Woof!" I feel so great! I'm in a red mist and I love it. "Betty. Get in that room!" The door slams behind me. I go mental again on the tipped chair, barking furiously and slavering the glass, as Yodel Boo Hoo man passes the window. Alfie enters holding a Boo Hoo package addressed to Daisy. I run behind him and bark at the closed front door. I run back to the window again to see the Yodel Boo Hoo man take off down the road. Yodel Boo Hoo gone. "Betty calm down. It's just a parcel" Alfie says firmly.

But it's not just a parcel is it. We were under attack by Yodel Boo Hoo man. My role is to protect and guard. I naturally kicked into action, did my job fast and efficiently. So quickly I can't remember what happened, but the main thing is that Alfie got the parcel into the house safely and Yodel Boo Hoo man ran away. Job done. It's a great job and I love it. Nobody trained me, it's my instinct - a voice in my head tells me what to do. These involuntary actions I find difficult to stop due to this mind-blowing head rush.

So here I am being told off for doing my job. Big Dog just looks at me. He doesn't do much and doesn't really have an important job to do like me. Big Dog spends his time chilling and sleeping. We go for walks together but he doesn't want to play. He hates me nipping him as I race past, but it's funny annoying him. We've lived together for ever, as long as I can remember. I was very small and Big Dog was even bigger then as he towered over me sniffing. Big Dog would eat my dinner after he ate his. Think he was a bit greedy. Even now I wait a few minutes before I eat just to see if Big Dog will come and eat my dinner. He's like a friendly old grandad.

Hey! Alfie made me jump on the garage roof the other day. I just legged it high and there I was on the roof barking at everyone passing by. It's an extension to my job. When I was small wearing a red baby jacket I couldn't even climb the stairs. Now look at me being promoted to garage roof patrol. I could get close enough to scare people whilst spraying slather towards them. "Grrrrrrwwwwrrrrwww!" They got to know me and crossed the road. It only lasted a few days until the job was done. The neighbourhood knew I meant business. I was stood down. There was even a photo of me doing my job on streetview. Job done.

Love my runs in the woods. Such a laugh legging it through long grass. Big Dog likes standing in water, especially on hot days. Not my thing though, water. He gets soaked and it takes hours to dry. The car stinks of him. Old shaggy wet dog smell. If it's not the smell, it's the floating fur balls that get you. I don't smell and my coat is trimmed. Oh we had a top laugh once in the Peaks. Robbie's dog belt snapped as I yanked forward. I was free. Free to chase and herd sheep over the hills.There must have been hundreds of them and I managed to get them all to stick together legging it out of sight. That was such a laugh. Twenty minutes of madness. You should have seen me! It was worth the bottom smack and telling off. Robbie wasn't happy all day. He must have got over it because we came here again climbing up steep rocks with Alfie. That was awesome, especially when we got lost on top of Man Tor, the highest point in the peaks. I could have got us down but Robbie didn't want to turn back. Eventually we were descending through fields full of sheep. I attempted to break free but Robbie's upgraded dog belt wouldn't snap. No herding today.

Over the following weeks there was an odd feeling in the house and I felt that people were talking about me. Robbie was sad. I could tell. The word 'go' was used and people looked with their sad looking eyes into mine. Was it me they were talking about? I wasn't sure. Jess gave me even more treats.

Sometimes we were left in the house alone. Big Dog just slept but I was either working on guard or playing with things I found. The stair carpet was fun trying to rag it to pieces. Big Dog didn't join in. Just observed. I noticed Daisy climbing the stairs and she was breathless. She had put on a lot of weight, even though we'd been on massive walks in the woods, and she was eating more than Big Dog. I used to sleep on Daisy's bed overnight and sometimes she was sick in the morning. But Daisy was the happiest I'd seen her though. One day she disappeared. I didn't see her or Jess for days. Not sure where they had gone until Daisy arrived home carrying something wrapped in a blanket. I was so intrigued and excited. It was my new baby sister. Daisy introduced me to baby Lily but I wasn't allowed to sleep or go in her room anymore. I'd sit on the landing by the black gate and wait to get a glimpse. I'd often go to the park with Big Dog, Connor, Daisy and baby Lily. I'd make lily laugh chasing sticks. She was getting bigger and could now walk. We'd had fun in the garden which had been transformed by Robbie into a meadow. It reminded me of our walks. I'd watch the gate for Robbie returning from the shop, sitting, waiting until the gate opened. Friends and family would visit and we'd all spend the afternoon and evening there. The garden sofa was my favourite place to chill on sunny days. Big Dog would get too hot and go for shade. When I climbed on the table I could see the street and Boo Hoo delivery man. I'd run inside to the window to beat him to the door... "Grrrrrwwwwrrrrwww!" After a few Boo Hoo deliveries each day I'd chill on my favourite cushion on the kitchen sofa so I can still hear the door. When Robbie returns to the house I bring him a shoe as a present.

As baby Lily grows she plays with bigger and better toys that we share. I rob baby Lily of her toy and get chased around the house and garden. It's best when more people chase and the more anxious baby Lily is to get the toy back. I mostly win and move onto something like guarding the house. Sometimes they try tricking me and knock pretending it's Boo Hoo man. "Hello!" I know it's a trick but I go along with it for fun. I jump on the posh chair and pretend to look through the window. They think they've won. I just jump down and nick another of her toys. Game on!

When I'm on my long walks in the woods we sometimes meet other walkers and dogs. I just want to play and run around with new friends we meet. Unfortunately sometimes they look scared. What is it with us? Do we look aggressive? We won't bite! When on the lead I like to discover things and I pull to get there first. Hate being behind. More times than not, we go on walks and don't see many people. So I just leg it and enjoy the freedom of having an open space to chase. Until I hear the whistle that means to run back as fast as I can. Then we repeat it a few times, sometimes nipping Big Dog's back leg, until I'm shattered. I always win and jump up and try to snatch the dog lead or runaround Big Dog nipping him even more. It's our game. "Stop it!" Back to the car. Big Dog would struggle climbing onto the seat and I'd leap into the back after I saw him get in safely.

It was raining and getting dark. Big Dog was lying on the wet slate tiles in the garden. He hadn't moved all afternoon even for dinner or treats. A blanket was placed over him and a cover to prevent him from getting wetter. Everyone went to see him in turn. I didn't see him again but the next day but I could smell where he had been lying. Where had he gone? I miss him even though he didn't always want to play. At dinner time I wait a while just to see if he wants my dinner. He never comes, but I wait a short time just in case. I'd like another grandad or friend again at home. I find myself waiting on the sofa for Robbie to come back from work, looking at the door. When he arrives, I grab a shoe and take it to him waggling my bum. It's my way of saying I'm really happy you're back, but where the f*ck have you been without me!

"Squirrel!" That's my favourite buzz-word. It makes me wild with excitement. As soon as I hear that word I freak out. Squirrels are bushy tailed rats that are so quick they can fly up trees, so I have to leg it at top speed, knocking everything out of my way to stand a chance of grabbing their tails. It's the tail of a squirrel that intrigues me - I just want to nibble on them. On a run in the park I can pull people up steep hills chasing squirrels - until they let go, then I leg it at full pelt. Too late. Squirrel gone. They watch me from branches above, giving me the finger.

On walks close to home, people are wearing masks covering their faces. The roads have fewer cars. It's very quiet. We don't go out in the car for long walks anymore. But this year has been the best. Everyone's at home more. I'm never on my own. Especially now that Big Dog isn't around. There's always someone to play with. Baby Lily is now running around, even taking me for little walks in the garden. I'm her personal guard and I don't pull her no matter what. Quick! Squirrel…Squirrel !!!

We started going on long walks again. Jumping into the back of Robbie's car. Just me and Robbie. No Big Dog, but his fur was still everywhere reminding us. We have fun on our walks, but I do miss Big Dog. We play sticks. Robbie finds one, throws it, I chase it, grab it and wreck it. He tries to get it off me. Too late. He finds another. I always win. He's   too   slow.
And there he was on the sofa. A spindly, skinny pup with long legs and narrow head. His fur was brindle like mine, but with a white stripe of white down his face. He was such a skinny thing. They called him Rodney. He was here to stay. I liked the smell of him. Maybe we could play together. Maybe I could train him to guard the house with me. I'd have to be so gentle, he's so thin. We'd sleep in the kitchen together. Rodney wrapped in blankets on his bed of toys. I'd watch him during the night. He'd wake up, sniff and lick me, wobble around the kitchen on his long thin legs, sniffing. Eat some food. Pee. Eat some more food. Shit. Hardly ever on the mats that he was supposed to. It was a game to him. I'm sure I didn't shit and pee as

much when I was young. This was ongoing and always an issue with the others. "Look what Rodney's done again!" And after I taught him how to climb the stairs, comments got more heated. "Rodney's shat in my room. I'm not f*cking cleaning up!"

He wouldn't listen to me. As days went by, he did it in every room he got the chance. Sometimes it wasn't found straight away. Sometimes days, even weeks. Rodney started to chew things as well. He didn't want to be trained to guard the house. Rodney just wanted to run around, chew, eat, pee and shit. He acted like a… baby! And it was my job to turn him into a useful recruit. Tough job for me. He kept getting into trouble. The shitting was nothing compared to what followed.

Now, I have to guard the house. And if the special chair was there for me to jump on to bark and growl through the bay window, then I would certainly use it. No brainer. I'd be at head height with Boo Hoo delivery man, the chair would tilt hitting the windowsill and I'd jerk forwards as if coming through the window. Mouth full of angry foam, teeth snarling. Red zone. The chair was there as a piece of apparatus for me to successfully do my job. Of course I got claws. And on occasions they would scratch, or maybe a little more than a scratch would appear on top of the chair. Eventually after many successful exercises guarding the house, a small rip appeared. Then two. The woollen, Burberry clothed special chair did take a little hammering from time to time. And Jess was very angry. Very. But that was all part of the job. A little wear and tear. A yellow blanket was placed over the chair and it was moved away from the bay window. Wasn't too much of a problem.

Being quite tall I can stand on my hindlegs, growling, head-butting the window with slaver.

But Skinny Rod. He took it a step beyond. It wasn't even part of an exercise guarding the house. It was pure destruction. Someone leaves the front room door a jar, then Skinny Rod will sneak on and shit on the carpet. This became expected. They always argue about who left the door open. But it's mostly Daisy, sometimes Robbie that has to clear it up. It got to the point where the carpet had to be industrially cleaned. The words "It's your dog!" were often heard. This time Rodney ripped the very special chair to pieces. Shredded it with his sharp baby teeth and long jaw. Cloth and foam covered the carpet, the newly cleaned carpet. But the chair. OMG. That naughty Skinny Rod.

OK, when I was younger I chewed up those expensive bi-focal designer glasses. Think they belong to Jess if I remember correctly. That came at a bad time because they'd only live there for a few months and Jess was low or stressed or whatever. They were only small. Jess got some more. Whereas this chair is big. Much bigger. And it was such a mess! That room looked bombed. One day, months later, that special chair disappeared for a while. Thought they'd thrown it away. It only came back better than new! Wasn't such a big deal after all.

Teaching Skinny Rodney the role of guarding has been a challenge. One, he's too skinny. Two, he doesn't scare- he just gets in the way putting in bluntly. Makes my guard job a tad harder. When I'm going mad at the door or window, he's barking at me! What's the point of that? Means I'm getting pincer-attacked. Guarding for me is now double the job. Still. I get the job done. Skinny Rod has started copying my greeting. He too picks up a shoe and takes it to whoever has arrived back home, but he doesn't have the bum waggle. Too skinny. Skinny Rod needs to learn about personal space. He'll jump up at baby Lily and lick her, stand in the face of people when they're watching telly, and kick me with his skinny legs with sharp toenails when I'm resting. I hate that!

Now he's growing up, I'm teaching him tug of war with a rope toy or a delivered parcel snatched from someone's hand. I let him win to boost his confidence. On local street walks, Skinny Rod still hasn't developed the sight skills of recognising the Boo Hoo delivery man on the next street. That will take time. I can spot one as soon as he gets out of the van, and I'm immediately on guard. To say he is a sight-hound maybe he needs his eyes tested.

Our long dog walks have totally changed. At the woods he's let off the lead first by Robbie. This must be tactical. Robbie wants to observe his actions. I walk on lead with Robbie observing too until there's a long clear space with nobody in sight. And when we see another dog walker in the distance, Robbie still calls me to go on the lead first. Often he leaves Rodney off the lead as we greet the other dog. Again, Robbie must be allowing him 'dog social time' whereas, I'm back on the lead observing Skinny Rod's behavioural actions with Robbie. Thinking about it, I'm always put on the lead when we see another dog.

There's a few places on long walks where I give him sprint training exercises. Skinny Rod will run massive circles through the grass meadows whilst I'll run in smaller inner circles then attack him on the diagonal. He's rapid. Nearly as fast as me but I don't need to demonstrate my speed. Good tactics always win. Knowing when to attack is the key. That's my favourite field exercise with him, running wild with Rod through brambles, woods, and puddles. The whistle will blow and we'll race back to Robbie. Sinny Rod can jump the gun. As soon as Robbie lifts the tailgate for us to jump in, he never waits for his command. Up he jumps without any effort. He presumes that's going to be the command. I'll wait until Robbie has to really shout 'jump up in the f*cking car!' A reminder to Robbie that guard dogs should only act to strong commands, and that he has to be more commanding.

Robbie gets it right when the Boo Hoo delivery man knocks at the door. I'll be in red-mist attack mode, barking making sure our defence of the front door is clear. Skinny Rod, well, he still barks at me. I have to tell him off with a quick friendly attack. Then Robbie commands 'get in the f*cking room Betty!' and slams the door on us. It's always a command to me and not Skinny Rod because we all know who is the real guard dog here. We proceed to the bay window to fulfil our defensive duties to hear the front door being opened, and then Robbie softly saying to the enemy 'hello, is that parcel for Daisy?'. Job done. When the child-gate in the kitchen is in place, I give the command to Skinny Rod to jump it, to defend the front door. I observe him getting it completely wrong. As the door is opened, he doesn't bark. There is no red-mist. That stupid skinny idiot runs up wagging greeting our enemy! And sometimes he runs past into the front garden. What a plonker! More guard-dog training for Skinny Rod. But I love it.

RODNEY

I was born to run. Even my birth date confirms this. The first day of the first month of the year. And I was born first in my litter. Yorkshire born and bred, built purely for speed. My parents were fast. It's all in the genes. Grandad was even faster back in the day. He was a pure Grey. Used to race until he slid racing round the third bend in a floodlit stadium as crowds cheered. Rain made the sand slippery, so the story goes.

When I first met Betty, she looked magnificent. Beautiful and strong, with a brindle coat similar to mine. Betty wasn't born for speed. I mean, she's not fat or slow. Just powerful. Betty was born to protect. As soon as I came through the door there she was, coat glistening, her eyes burnt through me. I wasn't scared. They were deep loving eyes that went on forever. Dark brown and black with a glint of light, like jewels.

We had just travelled down from Yorkshire. I'd been held all the way by Daisy as her dad drove. I could smell McDonalds and wriggled to the screwed up brown paper bag stuffed in the door pocket. We had plenty of those bags and cartons in our house in Leeds. We'd race to get the leftovers. Winner took all. Daisy fed me a piece of burger. Then I must have slept. Next thing I knew, there she was. Betty, staring at me. The rest of the family was there. Connor, Daisy's other half and Lily their daughter. Alfie and his girlfriend were there too, sitting on the sofa in anticipation. All were expecting my arrival. Apart from Jess. It was obvious seeing her reaction that I hadn't been discussed. Work to be done there, I thought. Betty looked after me at night. I'd be asleep on the right side of the sofa in the kitchen and she would be curled up perfectly, head tucked, looking at me through half open eyes. I knew she was there to protect me. I felt safe in my new surroundings. The house was enormous compared to my birth home, with three flights of stairs that felt too tall to climb. Stairs that in a few weeks would become my new playground to chase up and down, frollicking with Betty. She was young and had enormous amounts of energy, sometimes too much for me being so tiny as a puppy. But I would later learn how to out manoeuvre her when I realised I was born with lightning speed. For now, I had to eat, play, sleep and take in as much knowledge as possible. Being in a new home takes time to understand where and how you fit in. No longer was I the romping puppy scrambling over my siblings. I was the smallest, and lowest member of the family.

It wasn't long before I could go on walks in the woods with Robbie and Betty. Sometimes Daisy and Lily would come. Once off the lead I would tentatively run ahead, keeping an eye on where they were, learning about my new freedom to run. My bandy legs were growing strong and already I could keep up with Betty chasing through the meadow grasses. Her strength I would never have, but my agility to dart and dodge her was my advantage. Being a sight-hound I resisted the urge to run off chasing birds or rabbits. There was an elasticated bond that pulled me emotionally together with Betty. I wanted to be with her. What's the point in hunting alone? Getting lost.

For a child it's much easier to grow up wearing a nappy, being taught how to use a potty until using the big girls toilet. Puppies don't care and whippets with their slender build and enormous appetite for food can't help themselves. I do not have a weak bladder as they say but food and drink just goes straight through me. I dread the morning when they come downstairs and see pools of water on the kitchen floor or in the hallway. I can't help needing a pee at night. And the mats they put out for me to poop on, well, they didn't tell me what they were for. I still have the odd accident. We do go on long walks and runs but my body, like any athlete, has a fast metabolism. Lily at three, is still learning. I'm sorry to upset people in our home but I have to do what I have to do. I learnt that bedrooms are not the best place to poo. The tiled floors are the best option. Didn't really want to mention this but needed to get it off my chest.

And yes I did chew the carpet, cushions and I ragged the special chair in the front room. I was teething. My excuse, yes. To be honest, I wanted to impress Betty with my skills. Ragging the chair was wrong. That chair wasn't just a chair. Jess had bought that chair from Liberty in London for a fortune. And I ragged it to pieces. They should have told me it was out of bounds. Things aren't said in this house, just expected. I was expected not to chew, not to wee and not to poop in our home. That wasn't drilled into me. Now I am an adolescent and on top of things, even though they still call me Pissy Rod. I love my home, my family, especially Betty.

On training days in the meadows, Betty will chase me in circles. I let her catch me for a wrestle then off we'll go again. I'll scamper leaping over her impressively. Betty is good at training me. She'll run in smaller inner circles as I run on a grand scale, leaping over ditches, tree logs and puddles. Each day I'm developing my muscles to sprint longer distances. With a drink from the large pond we're ready for more exercises. I'm not sure if my speed impresses Betty. Sometimes I think she realises that I'm much faster, but she never admits it. When we arrive back at the car I jump straight into the back onto the warm blankets. Betty waits for Robbie to command her a few times. The strength is in my back legs. Once I jumped into Daisy's car through the driver's window from a standing start. Everyone was shocked at how high I could leap as a pup. I now jump over the child-gate from the kitchen to the hallway with ease. This impresses Betty, especially when there's a delivery at the door. Betty is trapped in the kitchen to her disappointment, but I'm no guard dog. Betty is the one that protects us all. I look up to her as my guardian and best friend.

ONE AND TWO

There were heavy footsteps. The door swung open. Hands grabbed us. Then total darkness. We were so scared, weren't we.

Scared? I wasn't. It was our escape!

Escape? We got flung into a bag! You landed on my head smothering me. I could hardly breathe. And then we were travelling in a vehicle god-knows-where.

It was our only chance to get away from dried up food, filthy water and that rotten cage. We wouldn't have lived through Winter. Do you know that?

But we didn't know where we were going! I thought we were going to die.

We didn't die, did we. When the hands opened that bag, it was time for us to hop it. It was dusk. Fields and hedges as far as we could see. We scampered along the edge of the footpath then hid in the long grass, hundreds of poppies swaying above our heads. We sniffed the fresh country air. It was beautiful. The vehicle had gone. We were on our own. Free.

Free! You say free? We were in the middle of nowhere. It was beautiful though, and we were together. Young sisters, alone in the wilderness, breathing in the Summer air. For a while we just sat, staring across the fields, watching swifts feeding in the sky, noses twitching, ears alert.

And then you started. What do we eat? Who feeds us? Where's my bowl of water? Where's my straw to sleep on? You kept going on and on...

But I was right. We didn't know. We'd been thrown into a bag, taken into the wilds and left to fend for ourselves, abandoned by humans. As dusk faded into night, those frightening sounds began. Echoing croaks, the whoosh of wings, blood-curdling screams, snorts and wails…

Sounds of real nature. That's all.

Sounds of scary wild animals that were going to sting, peck and bite. The raspy bark of a fox that loves to eat rabbits. Two lop-eared domesticated rabbits, abandoned by humans left to become a fox's supper. A burrow you said. Let's find a burrow. You don't just find one. It takes weeks of scratching, digging, excavating, insulating and…

OK! OK! I thought a wild cousin would let us shelter in their burrow. To teach us the ways of the wild. To go back to our roots, and be rabbits. Not lop-eared domesticated rabbits. No 'lop'. No 'domesticated'. Just rabbits. Like we once were. Like our ancestors. Living in the wilds, feeding and breeding, amongst this beauty.

We aren't wild. But we are lop-eared. That's what we are. Lop-eared and domesticated. And this beauty. This beauty holds danger. And what do you mean about breeding? Breeding with who? Our wild cousins? What are you like! We huddled together, and chatted all night. The wild noises coming from the dark became more natural to us as time went by. The chirps and tweets of birds became orchestral, something we've never heard. We stood on hind legs and took deep breaths as daylight broke.

Phweeeeee!!! Phweeeeee!!! That whistle. So shrill. Then the sounds of padded feet. A dog zig-zagging running through the grass sniffing. Another dog having a pee. Phweeeeee!!! Phweeeeee!!! Soiled boots of a human pass us by. We kept low. Our noses twitching, hoping we were undiscovered. And then the man's voice commanded "Betty! Come on. This way. Rodney! Here!"

And that's when we first saw them. The two dogs. They looked friendly but could rip us apart. One was well built and the other slight. There was something about them. A feeling inside me saying they were somehow alright.

Alright? A sight-hound and bull-mastiff... one's like lightning and the other's an absolute beast. We lightly argued about this, lying in the warm morning sunlight. Birds tweeted in the hedgerows and a buzzard hovered until out of sight. We hopped about sniffing for food, nibbling one thing after another until it tasted right. We were hit by that pungent smell. Danger. The dreadful smell of a fox on a trail during the night. Close by, two abandoned rabbits, chatting away under moonlight, oblivious of the hungry fox and his rumbling tummy. We'd been lucky. Phweeeee!!! Phweeeee!!! That whistle again. "Rodney. Here! Betty! Here! Put this on." The man had spotted me, sitting alone on the path.

I watched from the thickets as the man leashed the dogs then guided them away from you. You sat there and just stared. Sniffing the air. The dogs caught your eye and the man held them tight. But I told you. There was something about those dogs that felt alright. Down the footpath, they went out of sight.

We were hungry. Wild grasses tasted a treat but our bodies had been malnourished for weeks. We searched for an hour or so, then separated at the hedgerow by the cornfield. A young woman appeared on the footpath holding the hand of a little girl wearing a pink ribbon and Summer dress. The young woman spotted you on the edge of the field, slowly walked towards you, and knelt offering you food. You sniffed her hand and nibbled, being stroked. I watched as you were picked up, held gently, then carried away. Down the path. Out of sight, and driven away. I was stricken with fear. I wouldn't see you again.

I'm sorry I left you. It was somehow our destiny.

Alone in the wilderness. For the first time, I had to fend on my own. Scared and confused I just sat there until dusk, through nightfall until dawn.

I was missing you too. We had been separated and I thought of you, scared and alone. In the wilderness, the hoots and the howls. The pungent smell of the hungry fox passing close-by.

I hid in the thickets by the footpath. There was no reason to move. To stay there made me feel closer to you, but I needed food. Maybe one day I'll see you again, if the fox doesn't see me first. It was now mid-morning. The poppies were swaying. The birds were tweeting in hedgerows. Phweeeee!!! Phweeeee!!! I know that whistle. The two dogs, the skinny one and the beast. I hopped out onto the path. I heard human voices and a man said "You can't believe it. There's another one! Rodney, Betty come here!" I stared at the man with the dogs, following behind on the footpath was the little girl with the pink ribbon and her mother. Was this my destiny?

I told you there was something about the two dogs! They're all part of one family.

The man led the dogs away and the young woman approached. She was kind and gentle as she stroked my lop-ears, whispering to me. The next thing I knew I was wrapped in a blanket on her knee. The man drove. The two dogs scrambled from the back to sniff me. A sight-hound that's bred to catch and kill and a bull-mastiff that's a beast, they weren't aggressive, just inquisitive. The little girl, safe in her car seat, would learn to feed and care for me.

I just couldn't believe it seeing you enter through the garden gate. I never thought I would see you again. Two lop-eared domesticated rabbits, together from birth, abandoned in the wilderness, a dangerous place. Separated and now united. Welcome home sister, we'll be happy here. There's delicious greens, new hay and a clean hutch ready. Now it's ours to share and become part of this family.

Together again. Living in a garden, in a warm hutch by tall trees. We scamper and hop about the lawn, from apple to pear tree. It's fun living here, with lots of company. We weren't country rabbits like our cousins but really belonged in a family. Rodney and Betty, they're both mad as can be. Rodney chases squirrels and Betty guards the gate. They say hello everyday. The little girl gives us dandelion leaves, mange-tout and broccoli. The young woman, Daisy, is our destiny.

PIG'S HEAD

It wasn't a hard decision to make, a no brainer really. Posted on our cycling club forum was the famous race Six Day Ghent (15-20 November) and the following extract which most riders were already too familiar:

Six Day Ghent is a 6-day track cycling race held annually in Ghent, Belgium and is part of the Six Day Series. The competition consists of 6 consecutive evening sessions of track cycling. With 16 teams of 2 consisting of 32 of the world's best riders including World, Olympic, and European Champions who will compete in 5 disciplines including elimination race, time trials, Madisons, and more, these 6 days of competition truly are a fantastic thing to behold. As the racing unfolds, a DJ plays music with an electrifying light display to create a party atmosphere for an event with a difference. The Ghent event was first held in 1922.

Some of our club riders raced at London velodrome, and I had recently passed my accreditation and was one of them. A totally exhilarating experience every time we hit the same wooden boards that Sir Chris Hoy and Victoria Pendleton had ridden for gold. Our racing, sedate in comparison, to what we were signing up to see. About twenty of us had bought tickets for the weekend racing, but a smaller group of us decided not to drive via Eurotunnel, but to ride all the way from our village in North Hertfordshire to Ghent. Peer pressure took its toll with eight signing up for the challenge to take on the 261 mile ride, broken with a night's sleep in a hotel in Calais. Foolishly, in hindsight, I thought it a good idea at the time to ride on my track bike, a fixed wheel titanium frame with one 70" gear. A bike perfectly suitable to race on the smooth boards of the velodrome but taking on any hills would be a problem for my poor legs. On the Garmin route that had been mapped ready for us to upload, it seemed like a gentle rolling ride to Dover and virtually flat from Calais to Ghent. Apparently we were to have a tailwind to boot. Sounded great. One thing we hadn't really considered to any depth was the weather in mid November. But at least we had a kit check to fix any mechanical issues and extra lights for riding safety in the dark. On long rides we were all experienced with nutritional needs, packed ready on our bikes for the next day's challenge to ride to the Six Day Ghent.

The roads were frostbitten as we grouped at the local pub at 08.00am, our usual starting point for club rides. Without hanging about getting cold, we rode up the hill and out of the village, South, avoiding busy roads as much as possible. A route familiar to us all for the first 55 miles but thereafter, we were taking on the unknown. Riding as a group of eight, gives enough rest for riders in a through and off formation, well rehearsed on our club rides and chain gang training. By lunchtime we were already at Tilbury awaiting to take the ferry across the River Thames to Gravesend, where we found a cafe for lunch. The temperature was dropping and the light was fading. Inevitably, we had to take the A2 dual carriageway to Dover. Rain lashed in our faces as we struggled with a headwind, and our flashing back lights made poor vision for each rider. Passing lorries, threw filthy water over us and made us swerve onto the verge. Dover 22 miles. That was a boost for our morale, however we hadn't expected the mile long hill that we had to climb, before getting our first glimpse of the flickering lights of the dock and the blackness of the Channel. Once ascending, I quickly fell through the group being on fixed gear. Only Geoff kept me company, who had all the gears but ludicrously had packed in his 40 litre pannier, heavy clothing and a pair of brogues, 'to look smart' for the evening meal in Calais. Other riders' legs already rested at the top, we began the descent. My legs were spinning out of control as I strove to stay with the group, who were free-wheeling at top speed all the way to passport control.

Once settled on the ferry with bikes locked to each other in the hold, we looked for food. Within an hour we were out at sea, that's when our journey took a turn for the worse. The high winds created huge waves that meant the ferry was being tossed up and down continuously like a clown's yo-yo. It came over the tannoy that we weren't to venture on the deck, nor did we want to. Green faces spread through our group. The only remedy was to have a few pints. The wind and aggressive sea meant that we were to land a couple of hours later than planned. The docking couldn't have come sooner as it was getting late. The big issue was cycling in Calais after several beers. Martin had plotted the route, and led the way to the hotel only four miles away. After getting lost for an hour or so, we staggered in our cycling shoes to the hotel reception. We were greeted by the elderly French proprietor who didn't speak English. After seeing the cycles he took us round the back down a ramp, then unlocked the roller shutters to the underground carpark. What a sight. Lined in two rows were a dozen classic cars from the fifties and sixties from Lamborghini, BMW, Porsche to Citroën DS, all in concours condition. His collection was his pride and joy as he gave us a short description of each, in French of course. Our treasured cycles were going to be safe overnight. Already waiting for us was a hearty tripe stew in a slow cooker and a bottle of heavy red on each table with keys for our rooms. The proprietor opened the bar and told us to serve ourselves, he was off to bed. That's when we discovered the Calvados.

Cycling with a hangover was the norm for a few of us. The next morning wasn't an exception, just that we didn't speak to each other for the first twenty miles. A tailwind made it easy riding in France but by the time we came to the border of Belgium, it was dark again and light rain soaked through our layered lycra clothing making us cold. A wrong turn took us onto a motorway, busy with commuting traffic on their way home. Each driver blasting a hoot from their horn, waving their arms to get off, and so we did. Up the bank with our bikes on our backs, over a fenced hedge, into a farmers yard. The Garmin satnav was going crazy, telling us to get back on the main road but that would have been suicidal and illegal. We picked up a cobbled road plastered in wet mud, which took us due East, the right direction to Ghent. An hour later, the cobbles were beginning to hurt, and three riders had skidded and taken a tumble without major injury. Our protective eyewear proved useless with splats spraying our faces from back wheels. Arriving at the Holiday Inn, situated centrally in the city, was a joke. We weren't allowed on the premises until we had hosed ourselves down in the carpark with freezing water to the sniggles of other club members, who had driven there and were relishing in their decision not to have ridden. We couldn't grumble because they had transported our bags with clean clothes, and a trailer for our bikes.

Our first night at the Six Day Ghent at the Citadel Park Velodrome was upon us, with the points race, madison, elimination, time trial, super sprint and derny. The latter being my favourite with the smell of two-stroke exhaust, as competing cyclists gain speed up to 40 kph draughting behind derny pacers. The atmosphere was electrifying, with laser lights and DJ, the mecca for track cycling. We were buzzing and didn't want that night to end. A brisk walk into the city centre, we were downing shots of flavoured vodkas in the smallest of bars that only had room for ten people. With hundreds of bottles of vodka on shelves on all four walls, and a bartender using a long stick with a hook, to grab the highest bottles. Rounds of evil tasting vodkas of all colours flowed. Two local lads in the bar had just graduated from the university and offered three of us a lift to a cool underground club in an old war bunker. It would have been rude not to have gone. The only thing I remember was the three of us, middle aged or not, pulling moves on stage to techno house music.

Missing breakfast was a bad move. Martin had in his head the idea of a Trappist beer tour throughout the city drinking half litres of Achel, Chimay, Orval, Rochefort, Westmalle, and Westvleteren. The six Trappist brands authentically brewed in Belgium with the following criteria:

The beer must be brewed within the walls of a Trappist monastery, either by the monks themselves or under their supervision.

The brewery must be of secondary importance within the monastery and it should witness to the business practices proper to a monastic way of life.

The brewery is not intended to be a profit-making venture. The income covers the living expenses of the monks and the maintenance of the buildings and grounds. Whatever remains is donated to charity for social work and to help persons in need.

This was an irresponsible way to substitute food with strong beer, but an amusing way to get to know the City of Ghent. One bartender had us all remove a shoe, placed in a net and hoisted on a rope to the ceiling. An insurance against the theft or damage of the hand blown, ornate glass tumblers that the Trappist beer was served. An original and unique way to make Trappist beer enthusiasts return their pots safely. We also learnt that Achel beer had been stripped of the Trappist authentication due to no monks living at the brewery these days. It tasted great all the same. Wandering through the side streets we discovered a costume shop, Avothea with the phrase "Beleef de magic van theater" scripted across the fascia. There in the centre of their fascinating display was a pig's head mask. Entering the next bar, I hung back and returned to Avothea to buy the pig's head, or rather four, one for each of us. These well made masks were for theatrical performances on stage, and looked rather scary in nature. Boxed in tissue paper, I caught up with the boys in the bar, then presented the box with two pig's heads, a duck and a turkey (only two pig's heads in stock). This became the afternoon's entertainment for us and everyone we bumped into. Literally.

Saturday evening at the Citadel Park Velodrome Martin and I were still acting like pigs, staggering through crowds, peering in tunnel vision through the pig's nostrils. It proved difficult to drink beer with most of it sloshing about within the mask. Eating a hotdog was virtually impossible, sausage being squeezed through a nostril, mustard smeared over the pig's face. We had gone past the point of return. Trappist beer had beaten us, now unable to consider removing the mask. Man was becoming pig. Martin was throwing up in his pig's head. Being defeated by the hotdog, we slumped towards the entrance for the centre of the velodrome, where it was standing only and very raucous. We managed to lose each other within minutes. The packed crowd in seats turned their attention from the racing to our failing attempts to find each other, as we were deliberately jostled and spun around.

The official website of Six Day Ghent posted six of their best photographs each morning, capturing the previous night's action. To our amazement for the world to see, were two drunken cycling fans wearing club t-shirts, and a pig's head.

THE MAN IN THE RED FERRARI

Heads are turned as the red Ferrari 348 Spider's engine rumbles like thunder in the belly of the P&O ferry as cars, bumper to bumper, await to disembark at Dover. A young boy, head on arms, peers through the rear window of his parents' grey saloon eyes fixed on the private registration plate 1 NA 66 and then onto the framed prancing horse logo. Stripes above the badge in red white and green represent the national colours. The driver, short light brown hair and a ginger goatee with a moustache, looks anything but Italian. The right hand lane exits first. The Ferrari revs impatiently for lane two to move in turn onto dry land. Car windows are closed simultaneously to dampen the noise of the V8 engine. Exhaust fumes and mist from the early morning docking converge as the Ferrari crawls up the ferry ramp directed by numerous staff wearing hi-viz jackets. An LED dot-matrix sign reminds new arrivals that it's 08.19 TUESDAY 05 April 1991, others flash STAY IN LANE and PASSPORTS.

The twenty-five year old, Neil Ainsworth, leans over the passenger seat of the Ferrari, arm stretched presenting his British passport to the hand appearing from the first booth. "Thank you Sir. Please can you get out of the car." Neil half climbs out of the driver's left hand door as the border force officer studies his passport and face. "Thanks Mr. Ainsworth. You may proceed to customs." Neil joins the queue of cars and is reunited with the boy's eyes in the grey saloon transfixed on his car. Most vehicles pass smoothly through customs as Neil approaches. The boy waves goodbye as Neil comes to a standstill directed by a customs officer. Another officer walks round the front of the car and signals Neil to open his window. "Hello Sir. What is the nature of your journey?"

Neil begins to explain as he gets out of the car and opens the boot. "I pick up flowers from Marseille docks and drop them off at Boutique Flowers of Mayfair. Florists to the filthy rich. The Qataf or Sea Lavender is Qatar's national flower and grows along the country's coastline. Used for Arab weddings, ceremonies and family gatherings." The customs supervisor, Frank Wilkins, a man in his late fifties with over thirty years experience at Dover border control, studies Neil briefly and then the flowers. "Very good Sir. I hope you deliver your flowers safely." As the Ferrari drives off, Frank Wilkins catches the other officer say under his breath, "Lucky bugger. Must be a lottery winner!"

The LED dot-matrix sign flashes 08.16 TUESDAY 12 April 1991. Neil Ainsworth hands his passport to the border force officer through the passenger window of the red Ferrari Spider, then gets out of the car. He knows the routine now. Passport checked, Neil drives to the next booth. He recognises the customs supervisor, Frank Wilkins, from the previous week. "Hello Sir. Please get out of the car with your passport and driving licence. The procedure is slightly different but Neil thinks nothing of it. The documents are checked by two officers in the booth. The DVLA information tallies with the name on his passport and states that Neil has a clean licence. He is kept in conversation with the supervisor as two officers check the interior of his car. Again, the boot contains roughly the same amount of fresh Qataf flowers as the week before. And again Frank Wilkins wishes him a safe delivery to London.

A week later, at 08.23 Tuesday 19th April 1991 the red Ferrari Spider, registration 1 NA 66 was stopped by Frank Wilkins and his customs team at Dover. This time Neil is asked to pull up into the bay for a full inspection. Frank explains that it would take around an hour or so. The Ferrari is found to be registered to Neil Ainsworth, 37 The Ridgeway, Tonbridge, Kent, TN10 04TJ since March 1991 from new. The trip mileage indicates 1298 miles so far for the journey so far. All looks legitimate. A sniffer dog is led to the Ferrari, doors, bonnet and boot all opened. Neil observes his car being raised by a surface mounted lift. Spotlights shining on the undercarriage, the Ferrari is inspected by three border force experts. Again Neil Ainsworth is asked to proceed safely on his journey to London by Frank Wilkins, with yet another fresh load of Qataf flowers.

On Tuesday 26th April and 3rd May 1991 at roughly the same time as the previous occasions, Neil Ainsworth is stopped by Frank Wilkins and the border force team at customs. As before, Neil's story is identical to the others and likewise he is carrying a boot full of Qataf flowers ready to deliver in London. Yet again Neil is wished a safe journey and told to proceed without any inspection or delay.

On 16th June 2006 in terminal two, Gatwick. Frank Wilkins, now a retired customs supervisor, is waiting for his flight with his wife. Frank recognises Neil Ainsworth in the departure lounge drinking a coffee. "I never forget a face. I was the customs supervisor at Dover. Retired now. Must have been over ten, twelve, years ago. Early Tuesday morning for five consecutive weeks, you drove your red Ferrari Spider through customs. Boot full of flowers from

Marseille docks. What were you really up to?" Neil Ainsworth laughs. Picks up his hand luggage, ticket and passport in hand.

"I got to know a sheikh from Qatar when delivering flowers to his apartment, who had recently moved to London. He loved the national Qataf flower, a symbol of good luck when moving into a new home or safety when buying a new car. He also had five sons who wanted everything. Drove him mad. But he had to keep them happy while living in London. Said I could save him lots of cash for a fee. Import tax. VAT. I was smuggling new Ferrari 348 Spiders. He bought one for each of the spoilt-brats. Bye! Enjoy your retirement."

PSYCHIATRIST'S CHAIR

It's not abnormal to see a shrink, I keep telling myself as I enter a rather stylish apartment in the centre of the city. Abstract art decorates the sparse vanilla walls, a multi-coloured bust rests on a white plinth resembling elephant man. If I didn't feel at ease, that disfigured head didn't build my confidence in what I was entering.

Group therapy hadn't gone deep enough. I was amongst other people similar to me, sharing a similar problem. A relationship problem. But none the same. My relationship was different. The group therapist took me to one side to have a quiet word, whispering that it's ok to talk about my relationship in whatever way I felt comfortable with. The therapy skirted around the edges but didn't scratch the itch. It wasn't helping, so I dropped out. The only reward was that I was privileged to meet some earthy characters. Being a dropout, I felt like some kind of loser.

I half wished I was living in New York where it's normal to share more time with your psychiatrist than a personal trainer, or so the box sets I watch suggest. Having seen this on The Alienist, my iPhone was already recording in my pocket, so I wouldn't forget our discussion. My memory malfunctions these days.

This is Leeds. I'm not aware of any of my friends, family or colleagues who have been in my situation. Expecting a chaise-longue and a bearded aged doctor, my expectations were jolted as I was politely asked to be seated on a purple bean bag opposite my psychiatrist, already relaxed on its twin. She was wearing skinny jeans, white shirt and barefoot. Very unexpected. I was prepared for a Sigmund Freud lookalike. I felt obliged to remove my trainers, forgetting I was wearing odd socks. Similar blues, however sporting a different brand logo.

Do you know you are wearing odd socks?

Yes. I believe I do. I've another pair like this at home.

Often when people wear odd socks…

Sorry. Poor joke. I am aware. It's my laziness pairing them up. That's all.

OK. Tell me why are you coming in for an appointment?

I was advised to see you by my group therapist. A deeper 'one on one' rather than hiding away in a group session. I wasn't hiding, I was more intrigued with other people's lives rather than my own. And everyone seemed to go quiet when I spoke with little response. In the end I didn't say much in those sessions. I'm here because I've not been myself for a while, and I've finally plucked up enough courage to attempt to get to the bottom of things. I was hoping you might be able to help in some way. It's my relationship that's affecting me. Giving me issues that I'm struggling to cope with.

Why now?

Everything was fine for years, and now I wake up feeling bad and guilty. I'm beginning to realise that I'm too dependent. And that's where I find myself now.

Questioning how we should be in our relationship. Most of my adult life. Most of my best memories, we're together. It's been so many years. I'm not saying we don't get on now. We do… some days. We've had great times, and occasionally we still do. But it's the dark times, spending too much time together for days on end. Going to bed together. Waking up in the night by my side, and in the morning, leading to long afternoons, and evenings together. Day after day the same pattern. Then with a jolt we're apart. I feel glass half empty at best, often totally empty. Feeling low for hours on end, building to very low. Depression sets in. I start to question if it's all worth it. During long days at work, I feel awful. When I'm really busy, when fully occupied, I can trick my mind and forget about it for a while.

Why do you want to forget about it?

Because it's not healthy. Longing to get back. To be together again. Watching the clock, the hours, the minutes slowly pass. The longing, niggling, at the back of my mind. A little voice nagging constantly, "Come back. Come back." The therapy programme encourages independence, to liberate ourselves. Feeling happy in everyday life. Apart, that is. Recently, the more time we're together, the more those happy times feel further away. That's the problem. It used to be a perfect marriage for years. But now I don't know if it's worth it. We're together most of the time some days. But the more we're together, the harder it is to be apart. It's a vicious circle.

 Describe those happy times?

We could be anywhere and we'd have a laugh. We didn't have to be away on holiday or anywhere special, that said; Paris, New York, Berlin, Dublin and the rest. I had a good job in London that gave us the opportunity to have a city break. I mean if we were just together, in the park for example. Hand in hand. And funny enough, with others, it was even more fun. Felt right. Normal. Like an endorsement. A seal of approval that we're doing the right thing. Everybody having fun. Going out we'd be in our element. Life and soul of the party. Big nights. Up all hours. Long hard hitting weekends. So many stories. Like many, it began with Friday rolling into the weekend. Quickly became a midweek thing too. Occasionally, lunchtimes. Commutes home were more fun if we met up. Just couldn't wait to finish work. That's a few years ago. Those days were fun.

What about now?

Then it escalated. Now it's more of a necessity than before. Without that bond I don't feel myself. I'm a weaker person. I've convinced myself that we're stronger together. That voice in my head tells me. Feels more one way now. I've become the more needy one. Didn't use to be. Any excuse I'd be up for a laugh. These days they're less frequent. It's more quiet nights in than going out. Trudging to bed early, listening to podcasts, only to suddenly wake in the middle of the night thinking I'm alone. During annual leave, we spend too much time together. I look forward to it but the fun melts quickly. It's a downward spiral. In many ways I look forward to getting back to my work routine.

What do you want?

I miss those highs we used to have. The really good times were special. Suppose it might be age catching up. I'm afraid we might be evolving into that old couple in the pub who sit there not speaking. I've come for help because I need to be more independent, less integrated and not to feel naked if I'm alone. Just be myself again. Whatever that is.

What is special about your relationship?

We were madly in love without actually knowing it. Crept up on us. We used to bring the best out of each other, full of spontaneous good times. Wilder at heart. Working hard, playing harder. There was a deserved reward. When a stressful working week dug its heels, we'd break it up mid-week and have a laugh, before going back to work feeling re-booted. Not these days. It's just about stumbling through life. One day at a time. Not brave enough to let go.

What's your partner's name?

Alcohol.

UNCLE JOHN'S SEA STORIES

Below the clouds of smoke billowing from Uncle John's pipe in his antiquated kitchen come living room, I sat crossed legs on his sofa as he began another tale from his life at sea in the Royal Navy. Uncle John, an older cousin of my father's, had run away to join the Navy a week after he had finished his education at the local grammar school. An uncertain time with WW1 brewing. He was barely sixteen but knew that he wanted to travel the seas and experience more of the world beyond Barnsley. Now in his eighties living with his wife Auntie Jessie, who constantly covered her mouth and nose with her handkerchief as soon as he lit up his pipe. Uncle John enjoyed telling me stories of his travels and looked forward to our visits.

They lived in a terraced house five minutes walk down the road from ours. My mother would take me as a nipper after tea to keep them company. Often I was dropped off so my mother could get on with marking school books or visit the hairdressers. I didn't mind. Uncle John always fascinated me with his tales from the sea. In his later career he became coastguard on the Southwest coast of Scotland on the Isle of Arran. This is where he met his Scottish wife, Auntie Jessie. More puffs on his pipe, observing my anticipation, his thoughts flicked through his mind's filing cabinet in search of the right story for that cold and wet evening.

It was bitter that day with gusts of wind blowing rain in horizontal sheets, making it virtually impossible to monitor passing vessels on the Atlantic coast at the mouth of the Firth of Clyde. If the wind picked up anymore we were sure to see a distress signal or receive radio contact from a fishing boat in distress. It was that time of year, but fishermen braved the poor weather conditions to reap some reward for their efforts. It was a hand to mouth occupation for many of the fishermen. No fish, no pay. They were hardened men with no fear of rough seas. As coastguards, it was our role to help prevent the loss of life along the coast and at sea, by coordinating search and rescue operations. We expected the worst and hoped for the safekeeping of all. A few hours passed and the wind had subsided. It was bitterly cold, however, with less threat to lives. From the control tower, we could see afar and all was calm.

There were crackles over the radio. It was a fisherman named Tod Geddish. I knew all of the local fishermen and Tod happened to be a good friend of mine. He sounded excited and somewhat nervous on the radio as he spat out the words, "There's a Sea Monster!" His boat was only half a mile from the harbour and two other fishing boats were close by on their return journey. Their radios engaged, "Yes! We can see it. Looks prehistoric!" It was about ten feet in length, with a head 'the size of a Donkey's'. A large 'gash of a mouth' opened as it took breaths of air. Now these men were highly experienced fishermen and had seen the wonders of the sea for many years. Nothing like this. From the tower I looked through the telescope, tracked one boat, then the next and before I traced the third I saw ripples in the sea, then the head of what looked like a sea dragon with a ridged spine. It swam between the fishing boats in a triangular pattern. I could just about track its movements for a few seconds, and then it was gone. The radio cracked. "Did you see it John? Don't tell us you didn't." But I had.

And to this day I still believe that this creature could be swimming in the seas and oceans, somewhere in the world. Now some marine scientists say it probably was a leatherback turtle with exaggerated ridges on its shell. But they hadn't seen that creature in the flesh. Only a handful of us can tell the true story of what we saw that day.

One hot Summer afternoon during the school holidays, my mother dropped me off at Uncle John's for a couple of hours so that she could go shopping downtown. The kitchen door was open. He was sitting with rolled up shirt sleeves and braces, lapping up the sunshine. He opened his eyes and told me to go fetch a stool from the kitchen and join him. I noticed a small tattoo of a bird on his forearm and questioned him. Without contemplation or deep thought he began his story.

In the Navy we travelled the seas all over the world and for a couple of months we docked at St. David's Island, Bermuda in the Western Atlantic. There we dropped off supplies for the army lads that were stationed there. The Royal Army Garrison, they manned the artillery guns. There are no usable harbours on the South Shore, so we had to access a lagoon via reefs North of the Island to enter St. George's Harbour. Then through another channel that leads to the West into another lagoon where we could dock at Hamilton Harbour, the Royal Navy Dockyard. It was a welcomed break after being at sea for months, to walk on dry land and see our ship docked safely. The base where our digs were was pretty high up. From the thick stone outer wall, we were able to see the whole bay. The base was protected by a battery of Vickers guns that pointed out to the sea. They'd not seen much action but they were there as a precautionary measure. On supply duties we were able to explore the island in vehicles. It was beautiful. So tranquil with only the sound of cicadas breaking the rolling waves.

Walking towards the harbour on a sandy road, I spotted something moving in the grass. It was a seabird. As a teenager I had studied British birds in the field and learnt to identify them by spending hours in the library, sketching them and making notes. At sea, I continued to do so, mostly in flight but often on our ship's deck scavenging. But I couldn't place this one. A medium sized body and large wingspan with greyish-black crown and collar, dark grey upper-wings and tail, white under-wings edged with black, and underparts completely white. Like nothing I had ever seen before. The seabird was injured. I gently picked it up, holding its wings to its body so it wouldn't hurt itself further, and took it back to base. Sitting outside the mess hall smoking a cigar, was the ship's medical officer. He too couldn't place the bird, thought it might be some kind of Petrel. What he did know was invaluable. The bird had a broken wing and advised that it would take between three to four weeks to heal. He was as inquisitive as I was in finding out the species. First, it needed rest, food and shelter for a few days. He offered a store room that was quiet and sent me on daily errands to pick various shellfish and dead fish from the beach. After a week, the bird was seemingly much healthier and we had learnt about its eating habits. It became familiar with my daily visits and didn't think twice about snatching food out of my hand.

After two weeks the bird was flying from shelf to shelf. We knew that, because of all the droppings I had to clean up. By the end of the third week, it looked strong and healthy. The medical officer had discovered that it was a Bermuda Petrel, known locally as the Cahow because of the sound of its call. It was a nocturnal, ground nesting bird that was very rare indeed. For 300 years it had been thought extinct due to over hunting by natives and was now one of the rarest seabirds on the planet. After a month, the medical officer said it was time for the bird to be released. With a handful of fish, and the Cahow tucked under my arm, we climbed the stone steps leading to the artillery guns. There I placed food on the wall and it was released. Once the Cahow had a full belly, it fluffed out its feathers and just stood there, looking at us through beady eyes. "Looks like you've made a friend," the medical officer said. Once the sun had set, the bird took off out of sight.

The next day, I placed more dead fish on the wall. It was a warming surprise to see the bird return for its supper. This became my daily routine. Some days went by where I didn't see the bird, but I was sure that it was safe and well. As time passed, I knew our ship would leave St. David's Island on another mission and destination. One of my last evenings there, I looked out across the sea, deep in thought about the voyage we had in front of us. There, high in the sky was a Cahow. And flying diagonally across its flightpath, was another. I whispered the words, 'Let hope be with us.'

Now there are over 5oo Cahow seabirds nesting in the

islands of Bermuda and it features on the back of banknotes as the national emblem and symbol of hope.

HOMAGE TO A FORD FIESTA

Hearing the breaking news on Radio Five Live that Ford Europe had announced the death of the Fiesta after seven generations in 36 years, felt like a news filler. Surely there was something more important to broadcast. Maybe not. We've been drowned for weeks in the catastrophic failures of the Tory Party backed with sniping of the Labour Party. Maybe it was meant to be a light relief. Anyway, it provoked my reflections of our Ford Fiesta and the stories it could tell.

Ford's new baby the Fiesta Mk2 was the replacement car my father bought after my friend and I trashed his beloved Cortina in 1983. Sparkling brand new, it came with a bunch of flowers on the back seat as a kind gesture for trusting the hype buying this new model that only had had a mild facelift from the first model. Five speed gearbox, wraparound headlights made it look modern with significantly improved aerodynamics. It wasn't the XR2 which I had hoped but the bog standard, bottom of the range 950cc model. But it still turned heads in Barnsley because it was the new kid on the block. Bending down at knee height, looking through squinted eyes, the front of the fiesta resembled that of a Porsche or so I had convinced myself. And it was red, my team colours. All the better with the addition of the Barnsley FC sticker on the back window, which was stripped off for away games. With only 9 miles on the clock, my dad tested out 'what she could do' by inviting the family dog onto the back seat and driving to the club only a mile away for a pint. The clutch was keen but it was easier to park in small spaces. The orange disabled badge was an embarrassment when I drove it, but soon proved a great advantage when parking at football grounds. A small pay off. Within a few weeks, the back seat was engulfed in dog hairs and the turtle shaped air freshener dangling from the mirror couldn't outperform the wafts of a wet dog. Six out of seven days that dog climbed through the drivers door and slobbed itself onto a grey tartan rug that was strategically placed to keep the car nice. Fat chance. It stunk.

Having a disabled dad with a bad leg made me his personal chauffeur by default. The longer he spent at the club, the longer I had the car. The Fiesta's front wheel drive made handbrake turns easy, often over-cooking them ending in a 180 when on wet roads or snow. Fun for an eighteen year old with no lessons learnt from the Cortina escapade. The red Fiesta was fitting for my sister's wedding after hours spent by my mother, scrubbing the back seat to get rid of dog hairs and the smell. On that special Saturday morning, my mother also had to scrub and disinfect the pathway leading from our front door after I had had one too many with my sister's friends and thrown up several times the night before. The dog had eaten most of it. Sausage and chips with curry sauce if I remember correctly. The hangover didn't help my reading of clanging bells from the Corinthians in church but I have very little memory of that. The red Fiesta sat proudly outside, ready for me to drive my parents to the hotel for the reception. My dad hadn't prepared a speech, he was a more off the cuff kind of person who believed in his own jokes. He didn't disappoint his audience by being close to the bone with his humour. Later that afternoon, Barry, a mate of my sisters, grabbed me and asked if we had anything to dress the groom's cherished metallic blue Ford Escort. Tin cans on string was the regular thing but we had other ideas on the way. Parking the Fiesta on a pedestrianised walkway outside Boots, we swiftly ran in, giggling, and bought stuff and then into the fruit & veg market. The disabled badge worked a treat. Back at the hotel, the Ford Escort became a piece of art. Streamers and balloons were tied to every fitting, a potato pushed up the exhaust pipe and a symbolic dick was drawn in shaving foam on the polished bonnet of the groom's pride and joy, as he watched behind the curtain of the hotel bedroom window, unimpressed. The honeymoon was marred by the bleached bonnet sporting that symbolic dick that couldn't be removed even with T-Cut. The Fiesta had humiliated its bigger brother, the Escort.

Being in the dog house since the Ford Escort incident I couldn't dodge taking out my first cousin once removed. Basically, it was my cousin's daughter who had lived most of her life in Vancouver. She had been sent to England by her parents at the age of eighteen to discover her heritage. My mother and father thought that we should meet for the first time since we were three years old. To 'catch up' and educate her with the beauties of Barnsley and the surrounding areas. What? Vancouver couldn't be a sharper contrast. I was dreading my cousin's visit. There I was parked in the disabled bay at Barnsley train station awaiting her arrival from London via Sheffield. Without a clue what I resembled, she had been told to look for a red hatchback. A stream of locals trudged through the exit and there, nearing the last out, was my Canadian first cousin once removed. Imagine an eighteen year old Chrissie Hynde wearing long leather thigh length boots, a biker jacket with long messy but cool hair, with a bleached fringe. Stunning beyond all expectations, enough to make me nervous to greet her. My Townie attire, bleached jeans, cuts by the ankles, that partially covered my white Diadora trainers, a light blue Ellesse tracksuit top with rolled neck, and a football hooligan floppy hairstyle. My 'Hey up' introduction was met with a prolonged 'Hi' in a Canadian accent as she peered through her fringe. Bag thrown on the bonnet of our Fiesta, hand deep in her jacket pocket searching, she began rolling a fag. And thus began my five days of education.

The typical spread of wholesome food awaited our return and polite questions about her journey were asked by my mother. My father tried his best not to dribble food down his shirt and tie, the effect of his recent stroke. Carrying plates into the kitchen my mother placed fifty quid in my hand and told me to take her out that night, that it was better than staying in with them. I was used to making do with a tenner on a night out, so I felt loaded. My mother showed her to my sister's old room and I changed back into my indie style clothing to make us coordinate on the eye and in attitude. Knowing full well of my drinking habits my mother dropped us off at the railway station in the Fiesta to hit the bars of the City of Sheffield. With so many wine bars and pubs, I followed the crawl we had smashed on my mates birthday a few weeks back. The more we drank the more we bonded until we reached a favourite haunt where the UV bar uplighting shone through girls skirts. After an honest and brief description of why we loved this bar… she kissed me. That changed everything. The following four days were very educational for me. The Fiesta came in handy, especially the back seat. All good things come to an end. My first cousin once removed had a flight to catch back to Vancouver. Why had I left it so long to meet her. We could have spent the whole Summer together. Maybe that would have ended in someone's tears.

Back to reality. Barnsley FC had drawn Blackpool away in the FA Cup. My dad had been convinced to cheer on The Reds by a couple of his friends, 'to give the Fiesta a good run.' I was nominated as the driver. Cyril, my father, and his two friends from the club, Harry and Arthur, packed the Fiesta with thick cut bacon sandwiches, flasks of tea and walking sticks. The stinky dog blanket had been removed temporarily for the road trip over the moors via Huddersfield and the long stretch across Lancashire to Bloomfield Rd, Blackpool. The idea was to park close to the stadium and have a couple of pints in the first pub we could find. That was an eye opener for the three old boys. Performing on stage, wearing an orange Blackpool football top, were a couple of busty strippers. Awkward. But a couple of pints of bitter changed the mood. Onwards, towards the football ground. We set off with time on our hands due to the speed my dad walked. A steak and kidney pie and polystyrene cup of bovril went down a treat before taking our seats on the terrace amongst the home fans. Dad with the aisle seat due to his bad leg. Throughout the match the language was colourful, and that was just my dad and his friends. But I was used to that alright. On our return journey, Sports Report announced the result. Blackpool 0 Barnsley 2. We'd missed the second goal because the old boys always left 5 minutes early to avoid traffic. The red Fiesta was blown about on the M62 but made the entire journey on one tank with plenty of fuel spare for the midweek match, Sheffield Wednesday v

Manchester United. Dad didn't attend midweek games. He preferred going down the club to meet his mates. They didn't have strippers in that gentleman's establishment, or so they said.

As time passed by, the red Fiesta accumulated a deep dog smell that even a valet clean couldn't disguise. But that didn't matter. At university the Fiesta became useful for me and my college mates to move house and transport us wherever we fancied. Leaving our design award entries until the last minute, the Fiesta was our saviour. Preston to London was hell of a journey but long play cassettes with our favourite tunes made it fly by. Parking the car at Swiss Cottage and taking the tube was the best route to Pall Mall where our submissions were expected to be handed in by lunchtime. Relieved to have met the deadline we hit Soho for an hour to celebrate our hard work before hopping on the tube back to the tree lined neighbourhood of Swiss Cottage. That's when the fight broke out. Conkers covered the pavement and road, and once one conker was thrown, a full blown war broke out. With pockets packed with conkers, we used the Fiesta as a barricade as we chased each other launching head shots at full pelt. Once hit in the eye was enough, but being hit several times in the face we had to make a truce. The M1 beckoned. Passing the exit for Barnsley, we decided to call off and see my dad at home and then onto the junior school where my mother taught. She was surprised to see us. We managed to muster up enough conkers left in our ammunition bags to give each seven year old kid a shiny conker. Back at university, within a week, a parcel arrived. Enclosed were 32 thank you letters, one from each child. Our favourite, a scribbled drawing of a conker with eyes and nose with a crown on its head. It read, 'Thank you for my conker. I call it William The Conker.'

A few years later after dad had passed away, my mother would travel to London Victoria on the bus where I'd be waiting in the red Fiesta. On Bank holiday weekends, once a year a bunch of us would book accommodation from the National Trust book. From castles, a converted water tower, to a stunning medieval house in Rye. I would always invite my mother to come along, my friends expected her presence. The 15th century local pub opposite to where we were staying served the best real ale and had a vast range of Whisky. Sat in the bay window with a pint and a chaser, an elderley gent walked through the stained glass door and placed himself on the corner stool by the bar. The barman was already pouring his usual drink. As a child my mother would read poems and verses at bedtime by Spike Milligan, and there in person was the man himself. Made famous originally by the Goon Show on the radio. Plucking up the courage, I introduced Spike to my mother and a polite conversation was temporarily created. When asked how he was, he replied, "I don't mind dying, I just don't want to be there when it happens."

Our red Fiesta had seen life and enabled it. Even being the stinkiest car ever, she had served us well. Leaving our flat in London for a cottage in a small village in Hertfordshire, it was my decision to give the car to a colleague from work in exchange for a decent bottle of Speyside malt. That beautiful red Ford Fiesta served him well for yet another eight years in the heart of the East End.

RIP our cherished Ford Fiesta 1983 - 2009.

SEAWEED

The panting breath of the Norwegian Buhund was clearly visible in the early morning light as the curly tailed, stocky dog raced ahead on the Cleveland Way footpath towards Boggle Hole. Stunning views of Robin Hood's Bay, North Yorkshire, were once again captured by Professor Kristiansen on his Leica camera. Mist rolled over the sands and shale from the inbound sea as sporadic sunrays peered through grey damp clouds. It was to be another glorious autumnal day, the Professor's second of five days staying at a dog friendly bed and breakfast only a mile from the cliff tops. As usual he was prepared for all weathers, his dog, specially bred for severe cold temperatures. However, it wasn't cold. In fact it was mild which troubled the Professor and reminded him of the purpose of his life's work.

According to Professor Kristiansen's climate projections, the average temperature was likely to be 4.5°C higher by the end of the century than it was during 1971-2000. The dramatic and beautiful landscape uncurled his frown as he followed the dog down the rocky path descending towards the beach and the prehistoric cove at Boggle Hole, famous within the Palaeontologist community for its wealth of fossils. Storm Petrel, Common Tern and Black Guillemot scavenged the empty, freshly sea swept beaches in search of an early morning meal, the first of up to six needed to build fat in preparation for winter. With one whistle, the dog stood still and allowed his leash to be slipped over his head. There was a lonely figure ahead, what looked like a man with a pitch fork gathering seaweed.

The Professor had some knowledge of products made from seaweed and the local farming of kelp and other macroalgae. He'd seen a specialist shop by the quayside in Whitby that sold a range of shampoo, skin care creams, make up, shower gels, even yoghurt, ice-cream and toothpaste, mostly purchased by tourists visiting the area. Approaching the man, Professor Kristiansen studied his actions and piles of segregated seaweed. The man, now recognised to be in his later years with a weather beaten face, stopped and stared, pitch fork held vertically in his gloved hand.

'Good morning! I can see you're in the midst of collecting seaweed. I know it's increasingly popular these days in cuisines. The dietary source of many vitamins, antioxidants and iodine.' the Professor said in the hope of sparking a knowledgeable conversation.

'And good morning to you sir. Yes. We've been farming seaweed for three generations. My grandfather swore by it. Staple diet around here for years. People don't know how to cook it these days or can't be bothered. Couldn't stand the stuff as a kid but you grow to appreciate it. These days it's mostly farmed for cosmetics unless you eat in fancy restaurants where they serve it with clams. Nice dog you have there. Hello boy!'

The conversation soon gained momentum. Deeper into the benefits of seaweed, being a versatile product that can be used in the bioplastic, biotextile and pharmaceutical markets. Just requiring two things to grow, the sea and the sun without the need of chemicals, power, or freshwater.

'When you walk in a forest the air is fresh. The smell of fresh soil and lush greenery is both good for the mind and body. It's the same here. We're breathing fresh air. As trees absorb carbon dioxide and release oxygen, so does seaweed. See here, we farm three types of seaweed, each with their own unique benefits but all three have one thing in common. They're helping to purify the air,' the old man added.

The Professor and his dog left the old man to his work and continued their walk tracing the cliffs towards Robin Hood's Bay. Deep in thought, the Professor began scribbling in his note book. Diagrams, equations and numbers. Once they had reached the harbour, the Professor tied his dog to the railing and sat on a bench and began making a number of calls. 'If only we could… the conditions for spore reproduction could be recreated in tanks… the juvenile seaweed could then be taken offshore and harvested in three to four months… faster in hotter climates. Per square kilometre, it's potentially ten maybe twenty times as effective as a rainforest. It could be the answer… We need stats to back this up…' the Professor shouted down the phone with excitement.

Back at the B&B his laptop swung open and he began typing:
We can take carbon dioxide from the atmosphere and trap it in liquid form. Seaweeds do this effortlessly by exporting a significant portion of their biomass to the deep sea.

And then the Professor paused. He remembers the words of climate activist Greta Thunberg, 16, as she addressed the UN's Climate Action Summit in New York 2019. How ashamed he felt as her words fell upon world leaders and scientists like himself.

'This is all wrong. I shouldn't be up here. I should be back in school on the other side of the ocean. Yet you all come to us young people for hope. How dare you! You have stolen my dreams and my childhood with your empty words. And yet I'm one of the lucky ones. People are suffering. People are dying. Entire ecosystems are collapsing. We are in the beginning of a mass extinction, and all you can talk about is money and fairy tales of eternal economic growth. How dare you! For more than 30 years, the science has been crystal clear. How dare you continue to look away and come here saying that you're doing enough, when the politics and solutions needed are still nowhere in sight. You say you hear us and that you understand the urgency. But no matter how sad and angry I am, I do not want to believe that. Because if you really understood the situation and still kept on failing to act, then you would be evil. And that I refuse to believe.'

Never again, he had promised himself that he wouldn't damn the generations to follow by disregarding the sheer urgency by bending for economic politics of global leaders. If a local seaweed farmer understands the answer why wouldn't they. Scale. Scale, and even more scale is needed. A joint global effort growing and farming seaweed on a vast scale. Calculations were eye watering. It would mean offshore farms the size of Wales in every sea and ocean around the world. A fleet of ships, ropes carrying juvenile seaweed, planting constantly for five years, ten years. Forever. His conclusion was heartbreaking. But this can help reverse the climate crisis. There's no choice.

The UN's Climate Action Summit 2022 takes place in Sharm el-Sheikh, Egypt from 6th to 18th November. Its aim is 'to bring over 200 countries together to take forward coordinated climate action as the planet faces unprecedented heatwaves, fires and floods.'

Professor Kristiansen is attending as a guest speaker armed with the most powerful and most important presentation of his life. Will it fall upon deaf ears and blindness, or is it the beginning of our future, and for our planet.

FEET AND CLOUDS

"Keep your feet on the ground, and head in the clouds." A descriptive piece of advice given to me by one of my clients when working in London. "You've done well to get out of Barnsley lad." This I could have challenged for all sorts of reasons, but didn't, knowing that this particular client was from Leeds and in the top half of the Financial Times top 100 richest in the UK. All self-made, starting with his first credit card at the age of twenty three to bank roll himself. Thirty years on, one of the biggest stories in property.

The phrase has never left me and resides at the back of my mind. Words you'd expect to hear from one of the dragons on Dragons Den, poignant words dropping from great height, or a philosophical life coach, hand on phrase book. This client knew how to get the best and most out of people, demanding more than a pound of flesh. It was worth the pain. We had recently launched our start-up business in Soho and needed a secure founding client to kick start us in the first year. Now twenty five years on and out of the creative industry, I find myself reflecting on my career and life in general. All involuntary thoughts. So I've decided to break them down in no particular order, to find deeper understanding, flush my thought tubes, and put this saga to bed.

The combination of 'feet on the ground' and 'head in the clouds' is powerful. It's not an overused phrase combined but by no means new. Separately, I believe they aren't as strong, both very positive but potentially with weakness. 'Head in the clouds' gives me the impression of a space-cadet, lost in a dreamworld without a care in the world. Impractical and indecisive. Time being of no issue or relevance. On the other hand, 'feet on the ground' gives the impression of level headedness, grounded, practical and realistic. The two are opposites but compliment each other with huge impact. It probably was a throwaway phrase that my client used as a tool, nevertheless with great effect in my case. I will refer to chapters in my life as 'feet' or 'clouds' that may have influenced my ability to adopt this phrase, and realise it in real life. My end goal is merely to quash those niggling conversations in my head, unwanted non sequential sporadic memories, and live more in the present.

There are many contrasts and contradictions that pepper my memories that must have influenced me as I grew up, many that would fit into the 'feet' and 'clouds' analogy. At the age of five I attended a primary school where my mother taught, in one of the poorest areas of Barnsley. It's 1970 and even at that young age I could identify that other children in my class of twenty were living a hard life. It wasn't difficult to recognise. Bitter cold, wet and murky mornings, kids would turn up to the school gates without coats, shivering, and often even without shoes. Parents would half expect the school to provide clothing and most certainly milk and a warm meal for their young ones. The shoe cupboard was in my mother's classroom. Donations of shoes of various sizes, neatly tied together with string, awaited the shoeless. On the upper shelf, balls of paired socks ready to warm freezing toes. It wasn't a walk of shame to my mother's classroom to go to that cupboard. Those young poor children smiled as they tried on new shoes as if it was their birthday. We all got nits but some children also got new shoes and coats from the clothes rack. Nobody laughed because it wasn't funny. No one was taunted in the playground because many knew the next day it could happen to them. Fun was kicking a saggy football about in the playground at playtime, and eating together in the asbestos roofed dinner hall.

Twelve years later, in contrast, I watched the helicopter land on the school fields behind the church that we attended daily. A pupil of my public school jumped out, shoulders dipped to avoid the turbulence. It was the weekend prior to the first day of Michaelmas term. Bentleys, Jaguars, BMWs dropped off more smartly dressed offspring, laden with strapped leather trunks. It was an Indian Summer and excitement was in the air. Privileged, tanned kids embraced as they met, greeting others as they arrived. I hadn't got a clue what was ahead of me. It was my first day at boarding school. The Harry Potter books were a mere flicker of imagination in 1982 but now capture a similar emotion when the trainee wizards returned to Hogwarts. At the time, my only reference was that of Tom Brown's Schooldays, a book written by Thomas Hughes a hundred years before, watched in black and white on a push button, square screen television set, lying in front of the coal fire, when visiting my grandma in her mining village. Grandma, in her rocking chair, cat on lap. Parents, sister and auntie sat at the square table in the middle of her living room of a two-up two-down terraced house, eating tongue sandwiches and shortbread from a tartan tin. It was the money from my Grandma's house, when she died, bought for her to live in by my mother years ago for less than a grand, that paid for my education at public school.

The expectation to follow is not an unfolding of 'feet' and 'clouds' of the above because it's not that simple. Nor is it a rags and riches depiction. One being one, the other being the other. 'Feet' and 'clouds' were seeded from both contrasting lifestyles and culture. The tapestry of many experiences and memories in my upbringing certainly helped subconsciously shape my thinking and beliefs later in life. I'll continue randomly, as it does in reality.

Battered by an off-shore Irish sea wind, and horizontal rain, I squinted at the dot of a rugby ball kicked high in the grey sky. It's the Fylde coast and the school, originally built as a hospital in the 1840's, butted up to the sea wall so closely that windows were broken in heavy storms by shingle dragged by tormented waves. Boots filled with sea water and sand, I ran down the right wing and caught the ball, cotton rugby shirt now stretched to my knees. Into the corner, I scored a try. It was only a house match and that was only my first game of rugby union. The pain of the cold engulfed all our faces including the rugby coach, but no one could see the tears. Character building. I'd hear that more often as the traditions at the boarding school unveiled. Soon I was conned into a staged debating society competition: for and against 'ignorance is bliss.' Having a broad Yorkshire accent, meant in many persuasive eyes, that I would stand out. Arthur Scargill like. In favour. And ignorant. Admittedly, I was absolute shite but the audience laughed (with or at me, I wasn't sure).

Discovering the backstage hatch door was the best find ever. Barely big enough to climb through horizontally, we discovered pre-war cricket pads, hard backed arithmetic and geography text books from even earlier. And dust. So much dust you could hardly breathe. It was pitch black, even down the pit black, apart from a slither of light through the gaps in the wooden planks of the stage. We were the last year of boys in our Barnsley Senior school. The years below and the sixth form above having taken on girls. We were the last and lost boys. In the 1920's my father and his brother had attended the same school. Maybe they had worn the antiquated cricket pads scoring sixes after fours back in the day. It became our retreat from lessons we didn't want to attend. One afternoon, we thought it highly amusing to hide in there instead of attending the music competition. Not only was it hilarious looking at the whole school, shabbily dressed in shoddy grey uniform staring slightly above our heads listening to the headmaster bleat on how important music is in our lives, the two of us peering out the holes in the stage wall, sniggering. At virtually ground level, our heads were at the perfect height to see directly up girls' skirts, who sat on the front row. School is for education and we were being educated. Greensleeves, screeched from the school's quartet, never sounded so sweet.

Each Summer, between the ages of seven and ten, my mother banished me from home for a week, sending me to stay with Auntie Madge who lived opposite Grandma. It was pea picking time in the neighbouring green fields, beyond the grime from the local pit that gripped to roads and houses in mono grey. Picked up by a lorry at dawn, twenty or so of us would clamber in the back, illegally, and dumped in a field till dusk, without toilets or water. The packed potted meat sandwiches, homemade scone and bottle of pop, was a welcomed break from the line of workers pulling pea pods, filling endless sacks by hand. The village gossip amongst mainly women, who desperately needed the work, was unreal. It never stopped all day. A fuel that dragged them through each hour. Hardened hands, cracks in fingers busily working away at the speed of their gossiping.

The fagging system still existed in some public schools. Mine wasn't an exception. House monitors demanded 'toast until I say stop' and dished out house parades willy-nilly to younger pupils who stepped out of line. A parade in my house, Dragon and Crescent, meant twenty lengths of the swimming pool at 6am with the housemaster. My first parade was given after being caught with another couple of lads on the sea wall after midnight. We had dared to hang onto the cast iron handrail of the steps as the sea lashed over our heads dragging us into the aggressive dark water. In reflection this was most stupid but it was most exhilarating at the time. The early morning start hurt, not the swimming, but we were later fuelled, at 07.45 in the food hall with a full English breakfast, kippers and fresh fruit juice. The Victorian food hall had the capacity to feed hot food to all five hundred and fifty pupils, seated on endless oak tables, three times a day apart from weekends when we prepared our own supper. Parents would supply food parcels via post that filled gaps in stomachs. We ate well. It was an eclectic culture with a mixture of British and international borders. A sharp contrast to the mono-culture of a white working class mining community. Nevertheless, whatever religion, it was compulsory to attend church seven days a week at 08.30am before lessons commenced at 09.00am. This included Saturday which thankfully was a half day. Saturday was my favourite day. Pupils in school teams would compete against other public schools. Pride was always at stake and home games attracted crowds waving the school colours.

Throughout my childhood, my mother would cook breakfast, dinner and tea, served at set times. A structure that forced the family to engage in conversation, many during teenage years, developing into arguments around the table. If the meal was argument free, most likely one would spark in the kitchen between my mother and father whilst washing up. Pots were often broken. This took a sudden turn when I was fifteen. My father had a stroke and was bedridden, barely awake and speechless. Roles changed. My mother retired from teaching and became a nurse. My older sister had recently left the family nest and was living in Surrey at the foot of her forty year nursing career. I began to get into trouble at school and with the police. Being caught, finally, under the stage and on the school roof at night by the police and thrown into a cell, was the straw that broke my mother's back. My mother's hand-me-down college trunk was packed and I was sentenced to boarding school to be disciplined. A holiday by the sea, with strict rules and regulations. It was a bold move. One that in reflection, opened my eyes, and changed the rest of my life. Goodbye Tim, my much loved mongrel dog. Hello Nipper the black labrador.

Nipper was Dracula's gun dog. It chased me onto the first XI cricket pitch at midnight as Dracula's magnum naval torch searched frantically for the culprit. Lying face down, flat on the cricket square, heart racing, the beam of light passed by, as Nipper licked my neck, back and crack of my arse. With one whistle, Nipper had gone. I had escaped Dracula. For the time being. Having played rugby away at Sedbergh, a Roman Catholic school hidden in the depths of the Yorkshire Dales, a school with a fitness regime that consisted of repetitions of fell sprints laden with weights in a rucksack, we had to continue our celebrations of our rare and well fought win. Our school song had been sung in Latin as we entered the school by coach. School uniforms were ripped off, scruffs (non uniform clothing) scrambled on, we hit the official school club. A club strictly for sixth formers of legal age, run by pupils and enjoyed by pupils between 09.00 and 11.00pm on Saturday nights. Free from school masters and mistresses. It was our time. And yes, we did abuse the system. The bar sold only draught bitter, lager and vermouth with lemonade. We didn't wish for more. That particular night was raucous. We were cheered as we entered and Harry's were flowing. (A Harry was any free drink offered by pupils working behind the bar, soon to be eradicated by the Headmaster when stocks were taken). Many Harry's were downed that night. Enough to pluck the courage up to enter the Headmaster's walled garden, throw pebbles at his daughter's bedroom window. Claire, was also an attending sixth former and secretly was always up for a laugh. Grabbing the indoor swimming pool keys from the safe in the kitchen, Claire snook out of the house.

Diving into the pool naked was a celebratory ritual. Lit only by underwater lighting, I was still bouncing up and down on the spring-board and hadn't realised that everyone, including Claire, had grabbed their clothes and were running out of the back door behind me. Dracula was on the balcony in the dark, his bloodshot eyes observing from above, ready to pounce and catch his prey. The sudden realisation had me dive in, swim a length and in a frenzy, scramble out of the window naked, legging it through the archway into the square, and then onto the playing field towards the cricket pitches. Nipper was on chase. Followed by his master, Dracula, a house master who was constantly on the prowl after midnight. The following morning after church I was called into my house master's study. Dracula was also there holding a black bin liner. I was accused of swimming in the pool in the early hours. Dracula had a smug face, as he pulled clothes out of the bin liner. My clothes. My clothes with hand stitched name tags on every item. I was sunk. Honesty had always been drilled into me from a young age. And unless I was prepared to conjure some Agatha Christie styled conspiracy story, I was heading for the cane.

I never received the cane. But my mother received a phone call informing her that I had been rusticated for accumulative antics. It was my first term at boarding school and I was on my way home for the rest. It was sad to leave three weeks earlier than planned but there's always a silver lining. Jason Jones hadn't started his new module at Barnsley College of Technology, due to getting a job at the pit. Three of my closest friends had. After five lunchtime pints, I became Jason Jones and followed the group of students into a modest lecture theatre. These afternoon beer-fueled lectures kept me occupied for the weeks to follow until I was allowed to enter Lent term at my boarding school, having been disciplined.

Canary Wharf had recently opened and was the jewel in the docklands on the Isle of Dogs. Yuppies had snapped up lavish apartments but dropped like flies as the recession of the early nineties took its toll as interest rates soared. Gripping like hell onto our jobs, we moved into our newly built three storey house opposite Greenwich. Each floor with a balcony that opened onto the River Thames at its widest point. International tankers would turn around in the mist, waking us most mornings with a gutsy blow from the ship's horn. It was sad to hear of my Auntie's death but the kind woman had left me money most of which I spent on a 1965 MGB Convertible Roadster garaged beneath our docklands house. Great to look at and drive, it later became a pain in the arse, overheating in heavy London traffic, on Brighton boulevard and on holiday in Bois de Boulogne, Paris. But I loved her. The roar from the Wolseley engine as the overdrive kicked in, speeding with the roof down around the deserted roads of Isle of Dogs, a vast construction site yet to become the Docklands as we know it today populated by global banks. Life felt good. Really good. Definitely a 'clouds' experience.

The risk of driving my MGB to Manchester on a shoot to film a video for a new brand of mobile telecommunications company was too high. The comfort and power of the company's Audi Quattro was more useful, with a boot large enough to take all the camera kit and more. I say more because we did bring back more than expected. The Hacienda in Manchester Owned by Factory Records, was at its height of fame. During these mad drug fuelled years, boosted by music from the bands, Happy Mondays, Stone Roses, Inspiral Carpets, 808 State and The Charlatans, Madchester was the maddest place to be. Raving mad.

Four mates from my Uni lived above the Arndale Centre in a flat converted with old fittings from the skip when the local pub was fully refurbed, including the patrons name above the door. The living room now had stools at a bar, with pumps, optics and a pineapple ice bucket. Little genius finishing touches made the tap bar look authentic. Holes in the wall surrounding the dart board were made, left over bits of red Xmas tinsel stuck to the wall with cellotape, the finest of details. The flat was a pub. And it was also a madhouse. It was the prime meeting point before a night's raving and the smokers den in the morning coming down from class A's. And I was there to shoot a film with a crew from London. Richie was the life and soul of the party and a brilliant designer who decided Manchester was southern enough to live, coming from Cumbria. He also introduced me and the crew to a new experience. Only a week ago two Liverpudlian students from our Uni had frantically dumped a chunk load of what they thought was speed in Richie's flat. With the threat of a police trail, the chunk, the size of a large, thick chopping board, was smashed into powder using a baseball bat in the bath. Richie and his housemates were high as kites and subsequently had to cover their nose and mouth with scarves to continue the process. Now expertly cut and in wraps it was a race against time to get rid of it as quickly as possible. We were in the right place at the right time. The crew couldn't believe their luck. Testing the white substance for the first time, within minutes we were all off our nuts and ready to hit Madchester. Ravers on ecstasy, asked us what we were on. MDMA. And we were on another level. We were hanging on the shoot but it was worth it. A few days later, with the spare tyre hiding a bag load of MDMA, we set off back to London in silence. For the next six months, working late was a delight. Ideas were flowing, and the quality of our creative ability shot through the roof. We won many awards that year thanks to that baseball bat.

My rather dickensian upbringing planted substantial roots deep enough for me to understand rules of life. Not deep enough to be rigid enough not to break them. Being a creative director, you have to abide by severe deadlines, work to budgets but above all, be highly creative with both ground breaking and rule breaking ideas that can be delivered. As freud said, creativity lives on the edge of madness. He was right. Brands that disrupt the market are rule breakers. The people behind them have their feet on the ground, and head in the clouds.

PAINTED WALL

The realisation hit me like a juggernaut at top speed with heavy cargo. My time was going to be spent staring at a painted wall with a locked door. The feeling overcame me and panic very nearly set in. I just wanted to be home with my dogs, with my daughter and granddaughter enjoying the sunny spells and optimism that Springtime brings. But I wasn't.

My mind thought of Hannibal Lecter, how although caged and stripped of all luxuries and means of communication, his head was strong and he was able to cope with the thoughts that entertained his mind whilst in captivity. This fictional character helped generate my plan. Although there was no way out, there was an escape.

The power of the mind is based on the strength of memory. My memory was weak but recently I'd been having vivid dreams involving people in my life, often not related without any true connection. Deep down somewhere in the depths of my brain, forgotten memories existed, and I was going to dig them out. The painted wall became my focus, and my screen to project my thoughts. The mind game that was going to save me from going crazy was Total Recall. I began to conjure up themes from which I could go as far back and deep into my memory to the present day, creating lists of significant top tens…

TOP TEN:
BEST LAUGHS
BEST FOOTBALL MATCHES

BEST ACHIEVEMENTS
BEST GIGS
BEST KISSES
etc

After many hours staring at the wall, I'd collated several memories in each of the chosen categories. It proved too difficult to remember them in sequential order or debate them. The remedy was not to, but to have a rough idea of where they resided. Top threes became the new game, and I parked some of the discoveries of events, for the time being. Below are some of my favourites that entertained me the most to make time pass.

Having experienced VW Autostadt, the visitor attraction adjacent to the Volkswagen factory in Wolfsburg, with pavilions celebrating the brands under the VW umbrella, a spherical cinema, a tour through the factory, and the oversized 'sweet dispenser' where customers picked up new cars, we decided to take the experience further. We, being a bunch of designers, planned a Summer weekend driving to Trouville, Northern France, in hired original VW camper vans. Equipped with camping gear, music, essentials for the beach, and a blow up doll, eighteen of us scrambled into three campervans outside work in central London, to the cheers of the rest of the company as they waved farewell. Dodging through rush hour traffic in London in a convoy, heads turned. Especially the yellow campervan which had the blow up doll, sat upright wobbling away in the wind, strapped to the roof rack. The A4 to Dover allowed the engines to breathe in cooler air as the three campers raced at top speed to the docks at 50mph. The orange campervan seemed to have more speed, and began overtaking and undertaking the other two. There was panic on the driver's face and of the passengers. Off they shot out of sight. We hadn't a clue what was going on. The remaining two arrived at Dover but the orange campervan was nowhere to be seen. Safely parked in the belly of the ferry, the twelve of us searched the ferry for the stray orange camper. The ferry's horn blew, a clear indication that we were ready to traverse the channel to Calais. The car park was now emptied of vehicles. From the vehicle check in the distance, we saw two familiar round headlights speeding towards us. With much pleading from the driver and all of us on the open deck, the orange camper was allowed onto the ferry. Later we discovered that the accelerator cable had snapped whilst overtaking us on the A4 with the stuck pedal floored. Quick thinking, had one of the lads on the front seat bend down and loop the cable back on as a quick fix before they could stop safely to repair. All was well. So we thought. Docking, one of the girls realised she had lost her passport in the cabin of a heavy goods vehicle. God knows why she'd been there but it caused lively gossip. Nothing could be done, apart from hiding her underneath kit in the back of the camper as passports were checked. Free to proceed, we drove along the northern coastline of France, for what seemed like hours, before we found our campsite on the edge of Trouville, walking distance from Le Centre De Ville. The midmorning sun was blazing as we ambled down the promenade towards Le Marché Aux Poissons. Across the road, with a perfect view of the sea, was the 'Restaurant De Marché Aux Poissons, renowned for the best seafood in town. Perfectly seated on a long canopied table for eighteen, we took in the sea air and sights. Making it easier for le garçon, we ordered a large number of fruit de mer and even more bottles of Chéreau-Carré Chasseloir sur lie, Muscadet. We were still there sharing hilarious story after story until early evening. Battered by the heat and Muscadet, we staggered back to the campsite to get changed for the evening's rampage on the town. I have very few memories of that night. I remember losing the keys. Then being woken the next morning to the sound of waves, having slept underneath the campervan. Stories of that night unfolded as the weekend progressed. But some were left untold, with many sheepish faces for the arduous journey home.

In 2014 Barnsley FC were relegated from the Championship to Division One. A disappointing season but fast forward two seasons, it was full of blossom. Not only were we playing against smaller clubs that we hadn't played for many years, we also played the sleeping giants that had smouldered over the years and dropped into the third tier of English football. Bottom of the league at Christmas, under new guidance from manager Paul Heckingbottom, we had the best winning streak for some seasons. By the end, we found ourselves in the playoff final against Millwall at Wembley stadium to be promoted to the Championship. Only eight weeks earlier, we had beaten Oxford United at Wembley in the Football League Trophy final, a cup for the lower leagues but nonetheless, it meant silverware in the club lounge. Attended by 25,000 Barnsley fans, who'd made the trip to North London. It was a glorious day only surpassed by the more important game against Millwall. With no expense spared on my behalf, I managed to buy four tickets in Club Wembley, the best seats in the ground. Like all finals, it's the build up that's most exciting culminating in sheer bliss if you're on the winning side. My teenage kids hadn't really been exposed to the Barnsley banter and broad Yorkshire accent but at Kings Cross and on the tube it was raucous. Millwall were travelling from the South East of London and we were descending in force from the North. All was very friendly before the game but as you'd expect it turned sour grapes for the sore losers. Wembley Way was heaving like any cup final packed tight with team colours. Red and blue mingling together pushing their way towards the outer entrance. Chance had it that I bumped into old friends outside the ground, and at the bar my cousin and her family. The atmosphere was full of expectation as pints were gulped. Within 90 seconds of the start of the game Barnsley were in front and doubled their lead shortly after. Two brilliant goals that stunned both Millwall and their fans. It took another 15 minutes before Millwall picked themselves up and scored. But Barnsley heads were still high and full of hope. Half time was buzzing as more alcohol consumption lubricated the crowd. The next goal would be the decider no doubt, and Barnsley took the initiative and hammered in their third. Seconds after the third goal was scored, to our right, disgruntled Millwall fans gathered in the upper terrace. The angry mob climbed seats to attack the opposing supporters. That happened to be the family enclosure for Barnsley fans. Young kids, wives and grannies, looked terrified as they scurried to safety as if being chased by zombies. Coins were being thrown and then punches. Police were nowhere. Stewards couldn't handle the situation as fighting amongst the terraces escalated. A small number of Barnsley fought back, protecting their families. One Millwall fan was hit so hard he toppled down three rows of seats, which later went viral on YouTube. Police filtered the area and made arrests. Play continued throughout until the final whistle. We were so close to where the players ascended the steps to collect the trophy, we were able to shake hands with every player in the most exhilarating party atmosphere.

On the train the following morning commuting to work with a blinding hangover, I chuckled as I read the news headlines on BBC Sport.

BARNSLEY HAVE GONE FROM DUNGEON TO PARADISE
Barnsley sealed promotion to the Championship as two goals in the first 19 minutes set up their League One play-off final win over Millwall. The game was overshadowed by violent scenes as Millwall supporters breached the police barrier to force their way into the Barnsley seating. FA condemned the disorder and will work with police to identify those involved. Metropolitan Police confirmed 15 arrests had been made. Millwall FC will ban troublesome fans from games.

Training began at 05.15 most mornings. Open water swimming in a disused quarry that had sprung a leak decades before. The crane could just be seen above the water on clear mornings. Four laps, avoiding the Coots nest, equaled that of ironman distance. This had to be completed feeling fresh in the hope of finishing The Norseman Triathlon in Norway that Summer. Having reduced working days to four a week, allowed for long distance cycle rides and running half marathons. I was slowly gearing up for the toughest triathlon in the world. The Norseman begins with all competitors jumping into a fjord from the deck of a ferry near Eidfjord on the west coast, swimming in cold deep water, riding over five mountain passes, then running a marathon finishing on top of Gausto peak in the east. There are only 250 sought after slots each year, taken by professional athletes, Norwegian army, and crazy amateurs like myself who want to push themselves to breaking point. Training had to be slow and steady over the best part of a year to avoid burnout. Months of heavy drills and long distance training, each day eating like a horse and sleeping like a log. Some days were better than others. Feeling fresh was rare, carrying the previous day's slog and tiredness. I was longing for the taper where training time was halved leading up to two weeks rest before the event. Swimming with seasoned open water swimmers, cycling with a competitive cycling club, and running solitary was my tactic to better myself. I'd turn up for the club ride, already having swum earlier that morning ready for a six hour ride. This became a natural ritual on Saturdays, but it wrecked me. However it was misleading because we weren't climbing five mountains on the bike, replicating that of The Norseman route. This test was ahead, as ten club riders had planned to take on La Marmotte, a cycle sportive in the French Alps climbing Col du Glandon, Col du Telegraphe, Col du Galibier and Alpe D'Huez, made famous by Le Tour de France. Finishing fresh was my goal, with energy left to run a marathon. Fat chance. It was brutal. I could have cried falling off the bike crossing the finishing line with legs full of lead. No way could I run 100 metres, never mind a marathon. My club members didn't understand why I was so down as they all celebrated their achievement over dinner. It was clear to me that I was ill prepared and time was ticking before I flew to Norway. I took to riding a fixed wheeled bike climbing the steepest hills around

Hertfordshire making training more gruesome. Then up in the Yorkshire Dales for even more pain. Running off the bike was there to be cracked. I heard from a seasoned triathlete that I should time trial a ten mile route on the bike, then run three miles, repeating this repetition a minimum of six times. Nutrition was key. I had some experience having completed seven ironman triathlons across Europe but not in extreme conditions that The Norseman posed. As training halved, and rest commenced, my body was tingling awaiting the start of the biggest physical and mental challenge of my life. It was compulsory to have support on The Norseman due to weather conditions. My nephew had volunteered during his break from University. Neither of us realised what lay ahead. Bad planning on my behalf had us stay in a hotel six miles from the start but on the wrong side of the fjord. It would either mean a 120 mile journey or sleep in the car, taking the last ferry to the start line the night before. We opted to sleep. There was no sleep as nerves kicked in. In the early hours, race organisers and camera crew (see Youtube The Norseman Triathlon film 2011) gathered as they loaded the ferry, a couple of hours later, the first competitors checked onto the ferry. It was time to go. Like soldiers going to war, we walked down the jetty onto the ferry in silence ready to take on the beast. The horn of the ferry blasted and we were on our way to the start of the race in the centre of the fjord. The swim length had increased to over three miles due to the cold temperature of the water. The ferry was navigated to more shallow waters where the temperature was slightly higher to make the swim legal. We gathered at the hull awaiting a whistle. I was first to take the plunge into the black water. If not I might have turned back which was unthinkable due to all the effort over the past year and the expectation of others back home. We had been briefed to swim to the flashing light of a buoy which was the turnaround point. Every twenty strokes swimmers had to check their course. We no longer were swimming like a shoal of fish, draughting off swimmers in front, but solitary and dispersed, only spotting other swimmers when the surge of water subsided. Dawn broke as I turned at the buoy but I was shattered and freezing. 'Just remember your training. You can do it' the voice in my head reminded me. By the time I reached shallow water, aid was on hand to help drag swimmers from the water. A few athletes were in medical care wrapped in foil blankets with hypothermia. My nephew was waiting at the transition by my bike. Wetsuit off, cycling shoes on, I took a carb gel and off I went to take on five mountain passes. Big mistake. I was only wearing my short sleeve tri-suit. It was drizzling, a cold mist descended upon us and I had thirty miles to ride before I could see my nephew again to take on more fluids and energy bars. Miserable and freezing, I kept climbing on the bike. Hypothermia can play tricks with your mind, and I was very close to throwing the bike in a ditch. The mountains were high but not as steep as those climbed in the Alps. Eventually I'd reached the top and was on the long descent, freewheeling as much as possible to conserve energy. There was a camaraderie amongst athletes as we exchanged places on the road, always passing with an encouraging flick of the hand. The Norseman isn't a race against others, but one versus the elements and of course oneself. The sun rose above our helmets, and temperatures rose. I felt good. Having grabbed more gels and energy drink from the boot of the car which was already open for me, off I rode again to take on the other four climbs. Norway was beautiful. And riders were constantly lifting their heads to take on beautiful vistas of snow capped mountains. Two, down, three down and onto the fourth mountain which was pivotal in my mind. It was the penultimate climb of the day. It was a long slow drag but of beauty, and I shared the climb chatting to a local athlete who had already completed two previous Norseman. Advice was given for the run, a marathon around part of the fjord finishing on top of Gausto Peak. My mind was occupied with the run as I climbed the fifth mountain. In transition, I briefed my nephew to continuously park the car one mile ahead so I could refuel if needed. This he did perfectly for the first fifteen miles of the run. On the sixteenth, we were climbing the peak and no parking was available for nearly two miles. The slog of the run slowed to walking as the gradient increased. It was now 28 degrees Celsius and I was rapidly dehydrating. Dizziness kicked in, and I had to lie down for a few minutes sheltering from the blazing sun. Finally I reached the car, the boot was open displaying fuel, systematically laid out like jewellery in a shop window. A full bottle, three gels and a fuel bar were strapped to my run belt. Mentally refreshed, whatever the pain in my legs, I was going to conquer this beast. Due to my earlier mistake, I was reminded by my nephew that we either had a 155 mile journey to our hotel or it was sleeping in the car. All other athletes and support had pre-booked accommodation on top of the mountain. With three miles to the finish I shouted at my nephew 'Find two fucking beds and lots of beer!' By the time I reached the finish line, totally wasted, my nephew had found bunk beds in a simple hostel with no frills. The cold shower took the heat out of my legs, the Norwegian sausage dish replenished my energy, and the cold beer sent me to sleep. I awoke a proud Norseman ready for our stunning journey back to our hotel. Without the rigorous training, without the support of my nephew The Norseman would have taken its toll.

Murky autumnal fog mixed with smoke from the infamous steelworks engulfed Sheffield as we approached the city centre on the bus from Barnsley. Back in the early eighties, life in South Yorkshire was turbulent with strikes gripping most industries bringing the worst out of society. Town centres were a war zone for drunken fights, and looting became an easy game with the police force already at full stretch in the thick of running battles. Music was an escape from the anxieties of what the future held. It was a time to live in the present and make the most of each day, so we did. Dressed in donkey jackets, punk t-shirts and Dr. Martin boots, we jumped off the bus at the station only to be greeted by the Pond Street Mob who owned the streets of the city centre. Skinheads wearing sheepskin coats, crombies, skinny jeans and boots laced high up their shins shouting 'Stab! Stab!' as they chased us. They hated kids from Barnsley and were not to be messed with. The three of us legged it in different directions, quickly losing them by dodging buses, running down alleyways and down the underpasses. We knew the score. A few minutes later we were united again outside the Leadmill music venue, to this day still one of the best clubs for up and coming bands. Tonight's performers were UK Decay, a punk rock band from Bedford, and the main attraction, Dead Kennedys, who had flown in from California who had recently hit the charts with the banned track 'Too Drunk to Fuck'. It was only six thirty, but it felt like midnight as we huddled amongst other punk rock music lovers waiting for the doors to open. A Ford transit van pulled up, out of the back jumped members of the band with DK painted on the backs of their leather motorbike jackets. We recognised the lead singer Jello Biafra as he dashed through a side door. Bouncers shouted to get off the road as the crowd grew, then the venue doors opened. We were the youngest there, illegally entering the Leadmill successfully. Concert badges were the craze of the moment, proof at school the next day that you'd been to the gig, and a subtle way to associate yourself with a genre of music. UK Decay had only one badge on sale, whilst Dead Kennedys had one for each launched single, 'Holiday in Cambodia', 'California Uber Alles' and 'Kill the Poor', and debut studio album 'Fresh Fruit for Rotting Vegetables'. Two of each were bought, just in case one was lost. We didn't attempt to buy alcohol that night due to being thrown out for being underage. It was too much of a gamble and a high price to pay, harshly learnt from experience the week earlier at the Top Rank Club watching The Undertones. Smashed punks, pogoed to UK Decay whilst others spat on the band. This action wasn't one of venom, though disgusting, but an accolade for punk rock bands. We'd seen this before at a Damned gig in Huddersfield which was shocking at the time. The lead singer was soaking by the end of their set, encouraging the crowd. How would a punk band from California cope? Lights came on, UK Decay vacated the stage. Broken glass covered the floor, stinking of a mixture of cider and vomit. Bleached spiked hair, mohair jumpers, pvc mini-skirts, ripped fishnet stockings, and deeply blackened eyes was the uniform of standout girls. Blokes, bare chested with tops tied round their waist or stuffed in the back of jeans, packed the bar, desperate for more swigging before Dead Kennedys came on stage. Lights dimmed, drumming engulfed the venue, a spotlight traced Jello Biafra and the crowd went mad. Straight into 'Holiday in Cambodia' and the spitting started again. Jello Biafra leaped from the stage and decked a fan and attacked another. The bouncers didn't move. 'No more fucking spitting you filthy bastards!' was heard in a Califonian accent over the mic. And there wasn't. This band was too good to upset and you were likely to get a good kicking. Two hours later, after three encores the Leadmill was exhausted. We had seven minutes to catch the last bus back to Barnsley avoiding clashes with the Pond Street Mob.

Becoming winners of the 1983 English Schools Hockey Cup was an achievement in itself but now we were representing English Schools in a five day tournament in Amersfoort, Holland. Being the goalkeeper, I had only admiration for the lads on my team who each oozed wonderful stick skills and speed. Saving two penalties in our final game, was my way of saying thanks to the team for all the magic on the pitch they had displayed throughout all games. Calculations were quickly made, and we had won the tournament on goal difference. There was a thirteen hour ferry crossing ahead of us the following day, from Hook of Holland to Hull. Enough time to properly celebrate. Most team members were already of legal age to buy duty free alcohol, and it was done so in abundance. Being a beer drinker, I opted out from Vodka and bought a more flavoursome bottle of Pernod. Hidden in kit bags smuggled into the ship's bar, we took over a seating area awaiting for the Stena Line Disco to start. The dance floor became instantly packed full of other youths on trips, as the latest chart hit 'Ninety-nine Red Balloons' was lit by lasers. Boom! Swigging neat spirits out of bottles, we mingled, and danced with the party. A group of girls to our left were constantly exchanging glances. Without nerves, three of our team went across and politely dragged them onto the dance floor to Wham's 'Bad Boys'. A more reserved girl sat observing, so I plucked up enough Pernod fueled courage to offer a swig from my bottle. It worked and we began chatting. More accurately, shouting, above the music at each other, barely being able to hear our words. 'Words' by F.R. David came with a lighting change as couples took to the floor. We danced. It was a smooth crossing, and we strolled on deck to see other ships crossing under moonlight. It was nippy out there, and the air was damp so I wrapped my jumper over her shoulders not spoiling the moment. Our conversations continued with the background of waves and the humming of the engine. Then we kissed. A long teenage kiss that felt so romantic at the time, you can't ever forget. The film Titanic hadn't hit box offices, but in my mind this kiss was worthy of the silver screen. A relationship had risen, and we were submerged in a close relationship for three entrancing years. Teenage love :)

Armed Metropolitan Police opened the locked door. My gaze switched abruptly from the 'Painted Wall' and our team of officers engaged in securing the building for a VIP meeting that day, stood down. Job done. Time had passed productively with fond memories being rediscovered.

CIDER MAKERS

Rummaging in the shed at the bottom of our garden, overgrown with brambles and buddleia, was like a time capsule, trapped but now released. I'd managed to prise open a stubborn rusted padlock which snapped with the force. We had recently moved into the house which had been left virtually untouched since the salvage company had ripped out anything of value over a year ago. The property had been on the market since the owner, an old lady, had moved into a care home. We had never met her but her character was ingrained in the property. The kitchen had an old Aga still working in good order, the cellar had coal dust and marks on the floor from the shovel, now resting against the wall. And the shed, packed to the roof with gardening tools and terracotta pots, partially covered in creeping ivy. Some, damaged by age beyond repair, others cracked or broken by the roots of wild plant life. Ripping through the debris, I discovered a chest of drawers, stiff to open but intact. More tools, a bicycle bell, cutlery and decaying packets of seeds and rags. In the second drawer was an old wasp nest, a WW2 Defence Medal, and a small picture frame, the cracked glass covered in dust and cobwebs. Intrigued, I wiped the frame with the sleeve of my jumper revealing a group portrait of several people and a young child. They stood looking into the lens, the child holding a teddy bear, and by their feet lay metal buckets overflowing with apples. I soon realised, recognising the layout of the trees and brick pathways that this black and white photograph had been taken in our garden. Now midwinter and not a leaf to be seen on branches, I'd not given thought to our garden being a small orchard. It was a revelation, and quite emotional to think that we may be eating the same apples next Autumn. Once my muddy wellies were kicked off, I placed the picture frame on our kitchen table and went hunting for a penknife and magnifying glass.

Carefully opening the fatigued clips of the frame, the back of the photograph read Cider Making 1947. I held the photograph to the light and scrutinised each individual peering through the magnifying glass. Was the young child the old lady of the house? No, maybe the young woman made more sense. Or maybe she's not in the portrait. Who are these people and what's their story? My mind wondered if any of them were still alive. Possibly, was my mathematical calculation. That night I mentioned my new finding to my wife as we sat in the front room with a glass of red wine and a flaming log fire. She was more interested in the apple trees than the historic value of the photograph. But it didn't stall my enthusiasm to discover more. Laptop booted, I logged into Zoopla. The house previously was bought in 1935 and our record of purchase had not been logged, just the label sold read across the page. No other useful information was at hand. My next port of call was the Land Registry to check the title deeds. I accessed our property details and there we were, the new homeowners, and beneath was the vendor's name, Elsie Lois Burton. Having had our solicitor's doing most of the leg work this was the first time I had really registered this name in my mind. I held the photograph, and wondered if Elsie was there.

The following day a moment of pure serendipity happened. Buying a few bits and pieces in the local store I mentioned that we had recently moved into our new home further up the road. The lady serving me knew our house, the apple trees, and more importantly Elsie. She knew time had taken its toll, that Elsie had moved to Wellspring Care Home only ten minutes drive away, and that she was still doing The Telegraph crossword each day when last updated. A quick phone call with the manager of the care home explaining about the photograph had me waiting in anticipation for Elsie's reply. Only hours later the manager called saying that Elsie would be happy to meet me and was excited about the forgotten picture from 1947, and the people it contained. After polishing up the frame and replacing the photo with a fresh backing, off I drove to Wellspring Care Home. Reuniting Elsie with her lost past felt the right thing to do, rather than finding the picture frame being sold at some car boot sale for next to nothing.

Elsie was sitting upright by the bay window in a grand room with a high ceiling, and ornate chandelier to match. The care home manager introduced me then moved a chair for me to sit opposite. Elsie said that she had seen me walk through the garden to reception and asked why I wasn't wearing a coat on this cold day. The squirrels had been foraging and I had disturbed them but they'll be back, she explained. They always come back. A few words introducing myself and the manager left us to our conversation. As I handed Elsie the photograph in the restored frame, she slowly reached for her glasses, and began her journey back to 1947.

" It was my father's birthday. We'd been gathering apples all morning ready for the scratter and the press. We always made cider in the Autumn ever since I can remember. That's me on the right. So young. Must have been eighteen because I was back from college for the weekend. I had to run from the camera to take my position. My baby cousin Fi wouldn't sit still. Kept playing with Uncle John's puppy. Look at her. Fidget-bottom. Poor thing. We lost her not long after to Polio. And that's Auntie Mary and Uncle John. He never recovered from Fi. Drank himself to death and left my auntie heartbroken. That's mother and father, and my older brother Frank. He survived the frontlines. Our village was a 'Doubly Thankful Village' but still he came back a ghost of himself. Lost the sparkle in his eye. Hardly ever spoke a word at all. Just smiled. Unless we went to the races. He came alive then. We were born at home. Your new home. Lived there most of my life apart from a few years when I worked as a paediatrician at Great Ormonds. Then I moved back home, and converted the front room and the library into a surgery. Children were so malnourished. Good food was scarce and expensive. We always had a bowl full of fruit from the garden for the little patients. And a cupboard full of toys and games.

I could see that Elsie was becoming emotional or maybe tired. So I held her hand, closing her fingers on the picture frame, said thank you for sharing your family history, and maybe next Autumn we can make cider together with my family. Elsie said she would love that.

OUR SECRET (garden)

Across the busy road opposite our house, through a tall Victorian wrought iron gate, locked by a fiercely cold and rusted padlock, we enter. Down a narrow footpath encased with overshadowing hedgerows on either side and then a footpath that's even dark in the height of Summer, lies our secret. A secret that has been promised and kept well over a century. It hasn't always been ours, but a secret kept by many people over decades. Shared together through history, the same love and passion that it contains.

An escape from the bustling noise of city life, to tranquil, natural sounds and smells. Blue tits, great tits, robins and wrens eat from feeders whilst the cackling magpies await their pickings. A squirrel scampers to avoid eye contact with our dogs, smart enough to know that there's always an escape. Frogs are hiding in the pond's fringe, and just beyond, crocuses are indicating that Spring is on its way. The dogs bark. An anonymous shadow of a person walks by, seen through the hedgerows. It's quiet again, just the sounds of chirruping birds above the faint hum of the city and voices of children playing in the school yard.

Our secret was a discovery. One that we'd been staring at for three years through our window waiting to be found, but hadn't identified or understood. A secret we hadn't been ready to embrace and hold. Until now. After months of trimming, strimming, cutting, chopping, clearing, discovering, making and planting, we are now excited about Spring. What awaits is undiscovered as nature and weather takes its course. Undiscovered because we haven't experienced Spring or Summer in our garden. In the final quarter of last year, we were handed the key to the Victorian gate. Partially daunted and overwhelmed with the task at hand, we began our work.

Aggressive brambles, six feet high, twisted and gnarled guarded its territory. Its ally, the creeping ivy governed the ground with countless years of unrestricted growth. Uncontrolled sapling trees, seeded from their grand towering parents, fighting for light. Encircled with the overgrowth, the only source of light came speckled from above. However, beyond the gloominess and shadows, there was a flicker of discovery. There wasn't an evasive enemy to rid of completely, but the aggressors had to be controlled to offer new growth and life for others.

Within a couple of weeks the shape of the garden was recognisable, however, stacked with piles of various hacked, sawn and felled heaps of growth. The first discovery was that of a Victorian bricked footpath that ran from the garden gate, and with more ivy being savagely ripped away, the path continued and branched to the right. A hard bristled brush revealed the beauty of the red bricks, once painstakingly placed, one by one in a methodical order, giving a structure to the garden. The mind wandered with the thought of what it was originally like over a hundred years ago. Each visit to the garden, each hour of work, revealed a pleasant surprise, building the character of what had been lost. It was time to research, to discover more of the history and purpose of the garden.

I came across a Daguerreotype photograph with a young boy carrying a large pail, standing on a pathway framed by tall hedgerows, looking directly into the camera lens. Other young boys poised to his side, a lady dressed in a long Victorian dress and bonnet stands behind, hands clasped together resting on her apron. Other adults, smartly dressed in their Sunday best, hover in the background. Each subject knew not to move, as the exposure of the photographic plate recorded them in time. Forever. These people and maybe their descendants are the original proud holders of the 'secret' of the gardens.

Once used as grazing areas in the 1600s, these gardens became more formalised during the Victorian era and by the 1840s, the 75-acre site was established as "pleasure gardens" to provide space and an opportunity for those who lived in the city to grow their own food and to escape the confines of urban life. Believed to be the oldest and largest gardens in Europe, they hold such an important place in gardening history that a decade ago they were given a Grade II listing by English Heritage (now known as Historic England). There are 670 individual gardens on three connected sites: Hungerhill Gardens, Stonepit Coppice Gardens and Gorsey Close Gardens, now run by St Ann's Allotments' Association. They are a rare survival of a type of hedged gardens, found just outside the centre of industrial towns, which were once common in the 19th century. As well as the unique layout, some plots still contain Victorian buildings, such as summerhouses and glasshouses. (extract from Notts Live)

With consideration to how one normally imagines an allotment: flat strips of finely hoed earth, butted to a neighbouring strip, with a narrow path just wide enough for a wheelbarrow, canes precisely tied bearing runner beans, sweet peas with potatoes and a variety of other vegetables growing beneath with a shed in the corner- I concentrated on the thought of 'pleasure garden' from the article I had found. The shape of our garden is kind of square, even circular, with apple and damson trees, and an aged magnificent willow tree to one side. Encased with hedgerows and red bricked footpaths that create designated areas for vegetable and flower beds in one half, the other, an open space with a pond (a very exciting discovery) most probably designed for relaxation and entertainment. It was now our turn, to be the gardeners, and cherish this special historic place.

Making good use of the many heaps of branches and twigs cut from overgrown trees and hedgerows, we created half a dozen pergolas, from pyramids to circles, up to ten feet high leading you down paths, or enticing you to breakaway to other areas. Each pergola with a different variety of climbing rose. Six raised beds were also constructed, fenced with twigs to keep the dogs at bay. Composted soil, eight tons of it, wheelbarrowed with long arms through the Victorian wrought iron gate, down the hedged pathway, through our tall wooden gate, down each red brick path, filling each bed ready for the growth of wild flowers, sweet peas and strawberries. A neighbouring gardener said firmly, "Don't skimp on the soil." Advice was taken. Thousands of woodland bulbs carefully planted, a locally crafted potting shed erected in its original position, a pub table to eat and drink, and a swing chair to reflect on. Our garden was taking shape.

As Winter ends, and Spring almost breaks, new life is appearing as I write this sitting at the bench looking out of the window of the potting shed. There are things to do. As always. The birds and fish need feeding again, the hedges trimming before birds nest, and it's time to add manure. It's our first year, the first of many to come.

Watching my granddaughter help sow seeds, pricking out and planting, growing to maturity. Observing the garden evolve from season to season, year upon year, as the countless generations have done so before us. We already love our garden, a place free from the ups and downs of life, politics, and war. A place to share with others- unlocking the secret of the garden for generations to come. The secret, as we have discovered, is not just a place, it lives and grows in your heart.

TROUBLES

Jack was sixteen when his apprenticeship started at East Yard, Belfast. Like his father, he too was joining the generations of skilled fitters and repair engineers at Harland and Wolff. It's January 1971 and what was meant to be the beginning of an exciting career was badly scarred by sectarianism. The firm's workforce was predominantly Protestant, and Catholic workers had recently been subjected to intimidation, threats and beatings. The management was slow at addressing community issues that had angrily resurfaced, with reports of workers being thrown in the dock and pelted by Belfast confetti (sawn off rivets). Rumours were the least of Jack's worries. Mobs from Skankill Road rampaged the streets of West Belfast, smashing windows and causing mayhem. Women and children fled their homes and gathered in the hall of St Michael's church. It was becoming a war zone with an enemy hidden within the community, uncertain who the aggressors were or when they were going to attack. But they were, on a regular basis. Stolen buses at gunpoint, burnt out by incendiaries, acted as barricades on street junctions. Snipers awaited soldiers who attempted to cross sectarian boundaries, making them no-go areas. Soldiers began to occupy strategic positions on the streets. Checkpoints were activated in rife areas. This was life in West Belfast, and Jack wanted a chance to learn his trade and stay alive with his family.

It was dark and bitterly cold by the time Jack got home from the dockyard. His father had already sold furniture from their home, and was boarding up their front windows. Both parents had lived in the area all their lives, but it was time to flee and escape the atrocities. Enough was enough for Jack's family. They were moving out, cutting their losses to live in a safer area. Sectarian conflict was increasing and there was no future in West Belfast in the eyes of Jack's parents. Even his younger sister had to strip her school blazer of its badge, due to attacks from other kids walking to school. Cardboard boxes lined the hallway, packed hurriedly with their possessions. Jack's mother held the family dog, a wire-haired Jack Russell as she opened the front door with tears in her eyes. The family worked as a team, in silence. The borrowed Ford Transit van bore the load of their worldly goods. The van's engine fired on the second attempt. Without looking back, they were out of there travelling on the M2 towards County Antrim. Checkpoints were ahead on country roads and on entering towns. The van was stopped, driving licence checked and on the second occasion the family and dog had to get out whilst a vehicle check took place. The village of Galgorm was the destination, where Jack's auntie and family lived in a terrace house, not too dissimilar to the one they had left. She had helped find a property for Jack's family to rent, for the time being, on the same street. Jack scanned the street as the van came to rest, a front door opened and a black dog meandered down the pavement sniffing. Jack's auntie, coat buttoned against the cold, wearing slippers, waved and gave them each a warm hug. Jack's mother fought back tears as she thanked her a hundred times for helping them. This new life was going to offer safety, but for Jack and his father it meant commuting early in the morning by train to East Yard, Belfast.

Within a few weeks, Jack's family had settled into their new environment, however, sectarian troubles were escalating beyond belief. Twelve died in pitched street battles in West Belfast including a Catholic priest who was caught in the cross-fire as he administered the last rites to a wounded man. In the early hours, two British soldiers were killed in a carefully planned ambush on an army patrol vehicle. The British Government had introduced detention and internment without court hearings, and troops had captured several well known figures. Rumours of torture from these internment centres were fuelling public outrage. It was also spilling deeper into working life, now a battleground for Jack and his father to witness. Tension was high. Countless Catholic workers had left East Yard due to continuing threats. Jack's strategy was to keep his head down, work hard, and never to socialise out of his apprenticeship group. It seemed to be working. One evening when he was clocking out, there was an argument between a small group of workers. The words 'he's a fucking sloper' were shouted as a man was repeatedly punched, (sloper was a name given to someone who slopes off and gets someone else to clock them out). Jack, parka hood covering his face, walked straight by, unnoticed.

A few days later, Jack anonymously left the dockyard in the shadows then headed towards the train station. He noticed the girl from the payroll office ahead. She had helped the new apprentices sign official paperwork in their first week. Softly spoken and kind, with her long dark hair, pale skin and pretty face. Jack couldn't forget her. As they neared the station, three men encircled the girl. One prodded her collarbone calling her a 'grasser'. She looked shocked. Without hesitation, Jack intervened trying to diffuse the situation, then by standing in front protecting the girl.

There was an exchange of angry words, then a punch struck Jack. Two punches. Three. Jack held his ground and didn't retaliate. Shouts from others approaching the station made the three men disperse. One turned and pointed at Jack, 'I'll have you'. The girl from payroll reached into her coat pocket, then dabbed blood from Jack's lower lip with her handkerchief. Emma, he found out, had been working late and usually took the slightly earlier train home to neighbouring Ballymena. They climbed onto the packed train and stood opposite each other by the door. The window half pulled down, a relief from the streaming clouds from the smoker's carriage. Emma had recently been earmarked for disclosing names of known slopers. A recent crackdown by orders from management and the police. Several of the slopers had been involved in atrocities in West Belfast and were using the cover as an alibi. Jack didn't want to know who they were, just to stay invisible. Before he knew it, Emma had already invited Jack for a drink in The Crosskeys to say thank you, a local haunt of hers in Antrim. She didn't mention names of the slopers, but mentioned the nickname, Ghost, the man that prodded her aggressively and struck Jack. Talk then turned to lighter subjects and the evening ended in a small kiss on his cheek as they said their goodbyes. Jack was walking on air. As time passed, Jack and Emma grew closer together, spending many hours chatting over drinks in the pub, but never at home. Times had changed. They both knew that sectarian views would make their relationship abrupt, once their parents learned of their opposing religious backgrounds. Jack and Emma, despite the challenging environment, were beginning to fall in love.

On leaving work one evening, a car with two men crawled alongside Emma. The passenger door opened and a man climbed out, revealing the grip of a Webley revolver inside his jacket. He dragged her onto the back seat. The car sped off. A few streets later it stopped. The gun was pointed at Emma's head, and names of slopers demanded. Emma was staring death in the face. She was too young to die, in a war that she didn't believe in. Names were given as tears rolled down her cheeks. The door opened and Emma was thrown out of the car. In a state of despair, she waited for Jack in The Crosskeys. As soon as their eyes met, Jack knew something bad had happened. Jack listened in shock.

Thursday morning was particularly cold and grey. Jack and Emma had taken an early commuter train to Belfast as usual. But this time, with single tickets for the ferry crossing to Liverpool. Without members of the family knowing, Jack and Emma whispered their final goodbye to the Troubles.

OUT OF OFFICE

Working as a specialist at a design agency in central London can be quite hectic and very long days. Once a year our managing director financed our team away day to free our minds of stress and bond as a team. "Get out of London. Open your lungs! Come back full of creative life!" It was August in the mid-nineties and we were in the middle of a heatwave. The underground was a heaving sweltering pit. Corporate air conditioning was draining the London power supply. Power cuts happened frequently as BBC news flashes reported the cost to City businesses. To get out of London for a couple of days couldn't have come more timely. The 'out of office' was activated.

We planned to meet at Waterloo station at 07.00am with outdoor wear and an overnight bag. "Wiltshire? Where the f*ck is that? What's in Wiltshire." 'Stonehenge' fluttered through our group of eleven designers as they sipped flat whites, and ate yogurt bars, on platform seven awaiting the train. Our carriage was virtually empty, so we spread out, headphones on, flicking through Creative Review or laughing at the Fat Slags in Viz Magazine. It was a bright morning and the wind rattled the open windows as the train picked up speed. Wasn't long before we were flying through the sticks, passing copses, fields of cows, and medieval spires. Being the creative director, I handed out the itinerary of events. A 'Mind and Body' events company from Salisbury had scheduled a 'challenging and creative' outdoor workshop at Bucklebury Farm throughout the day, finishing with a traditional Wiltshire supper and accommodation at the 'Cock and Bull' public house close by.

The day was peppered with fits of laughter (and tears in one case) as teams competed in various exercises from building crafts to venture across the river without getting wet, the tallest tower that you could climb, and a tree-top assault course. It was physically draining, and one of the event guys acted like a sergeant major trying to squeeze everything out of us. One or two found this tough and out of our usual comfort zone (swivel Ergo chairs and water coolers). By the end we were shot. The hot sun didn't help, I suppose we were too used to working in a studio environment on apple macs. Late afternoon it was 'beer o'clock'. The pub served the best wholesome food, locally grown and unusual named ales. The events company had done a decent job and off they went back to Salisbury. More beers.

Some designers staggered to bed but three of us made the most of our time away. We could sleep on the early morning commuter train back to London. Rounds of the finest local ale from Tunnel Vision to Piston Broke were sunk, and as the last orders bell rang, we squeezed in a pint of 'Funnel Blower'. Two local lads joined us at our glass filled table. "Watch out for that 'Funnel Blower' it'll give you the squirts! You from London then are you. What brings you down here?" They were friendly enough, earthy, and also inebriated. We didn't share much about what we did, or why we were there, in fear of the London snob-factor. They gushed out drunken yarn after yarn. Hilarious. Next thing, we were jumping in the back of their series two Land Rover to go for a 'smoke' and to spot shooting stars in a field down a hedged, single-track lane. Lying staring at the enormous dark sky, glistening stars and the moon, one of the boys piped up, "Hardly ever get people here from London, they go down Stonehenge on the A303 then off to Devon."

That's when the idea hit us. We had to do it. Drunk and stoned, everyone was up for it big time. We'd been working on an international Pharma' brand identity and had 'fractals' imprinted on our brains. "They're beautiful patterns of circular elements that are graphically self-similar but varied in sizes," one of us explained, forgetting our London snobbishness. "A pattern. Right. That's easy! Get that rope out our Land Rover then, and some stakes…" We had some useful tools in the Land Rover, but needed to visit Buckley Farm again to pick up our 'wooden stilts' we'd made for the river crossing challenge. It was late with no one around apart from munching cows, their eyes peering at us wondering what we were up to.

The moon gave us just enough light to crack on until dawn.

ALIEN LANDING IN WILTSHIRE   [Scientific reports: Despite having been studied for decades, the question remains: Who, or what, is making them? It was an astonishing fractal pattern. This one unmistakably demonstrated intelligence. The only question was whether that intelligence was terrestrial or extraterrestrial. According to National Geographic, crop circle enthusiasts have come up with many theories about what created the patterns, ranging from the plausible to the absurd. Some people have suggested that the circles are somehow created by localised and precise wind patterns, or by scientifically undetectable Earth energy fields. Many who favour an extraterrestrial explanation claim that aliens physically make the patterns themselves.] source 'Live Science'

SInce our 'Crop Circle' hit the headlines, the Wiltshire boys continued their mid-summer creative art for many years to come, replicating the same technique- using stilts to avoid leaving human footprints, a stake and rope to measure the radius inorder to create perfect repetitive circles. Each year the art became more sophisticated and even more mind-bending for the media to report, and tourists to visit. The boys never let on who they were. They worked incognito. Simply took the pleasure of being creative, and their work being scrutinised and loved by everyone. It was a mystery, one that lasted for years, until now. The Cock and Bull has never looked back and has truly been placed on the map. Bucklebury Farm has tripled in size, now known as Bucklebury Adventure Farm, and the flow of passing tourists turn their heads to visit Wiltshire, a county famous for 'Crop Circles'. Today, a pair of stilts keeps our story alive, hung on the wall of our agency, and always a talking point for visiting clients and new recruits. Our story has become part of our ethos and lives in the hearts and minds of every one of us. None more so than the proud MD.

DUMBASS

During the sweltering heat of the record-smashing hottest day of the year, where we saw house fires and grasslands burning throughout the country in the news, I managed to scorch the palms of my hands on the steering wheel of my sunstroked car. What a dumbass. Running my bubbling blisters underneath the cold tap had me thinking. Was this the dumbest thing that I had ever done? Squeezing crushed ice wrapped in a soaking flannel feeling sorry for myself, I plonked myself on the sofa with a fan blowing the hot air across the kitchen. The dogs were struggling in the heat, flatout gasping for cool air, tongues dribbling pools onto the tiles. They weren't allowed out during the day in this abnormal weather in fear of burning their paws. Nor did they want to go. They were smarter than me. Whereas I had stupidly blistered my paws without thinking. The dogs weren't interested in my accident as I bleated on to myself, mostly in swear words, studying my sores. They just peered occasionally showing the whites of their eyes, not moving a muscle. In an attempt to belittle today's incident, flashbacks to more dumbass antics engulfed my thoughts.

Asbestosis wasn't a worry back in the seventies when we were kids. If our football was kicked onto the roof of the school dining hall, up the asbestos drainpipe we'd climb onto the asbestos roof, then boot the football to onlooking heads beneath, ready for a throw-in or goal kick. This was only possible out of junior school hours, having been banned from climbing by the headmistress. The caretaker with his dodgy wooden ladders with the missing rung wasn't there at hand to get our ball at weekends. His house was in the school grounds and in earshot. But he couldn't care less, so long as we didn't break any windows. He hated Monday mornings having to sweep up shattered glass. Then get his nicotine stained fingers smelling of putty making his fags taste funny all day. We'd clamber all over that roof playing tag somedays out of boredom. Running and jumping on the corrugated asbestos until one day it went through. Smashed asbestos scattered the floor of the dining hall, each in turn taking a glimpse from above. In assembly on Monday morning we were informed by the headmistress that sadly there had been vandals at the weekend who had broken into the dining hall through the roof, then proceeded to cause havoc. Flour from the kitchen had been thrown everywhere, completely covering the concrete floor, with potatoes splattered on walls. And a pair of soiled underpants were found in the boys toilets.

Nearly ten years later in sixth form I'd invited a mate to stay for the weekend to experience real Yorkshire ale on an eight pint pub crawl. Seventeen was nearly eighteen, and I.D was rarely asked for at that time, so long as you said your legal birthdate convincingly. Something we'd all learnt from the age of fifteen becoming veterans at the game. We knew most of the bouncers on doors anyway, and if you humoured them each week they got to know your face. Win-win. As usual we had arranged to meet in town at the Magnet Pub that Friday evening. Six-thirty or thereabouts. I had one job to do before we hit the town. My dad had asked me to put his car in the garage before I went out. Fair enough, I'd used it last to pick up my mate from the station that afternoon. Dad had a thing about his car being safely in the garage overnight. A red Ford Cortina 1.6 Ghia, with only 23,000 miles on the clock even though it was twelve years old. The car that I had that

Summer, learnt how to drive and pass my test, and the car my dad took the dog to the club for half a pint in an ashtray and bag of crisps. That car needed a good run. Driving 12 mph for a mile and back, six days a week, wasn't enough. It needed a good spin and I was in the mood to show off my new driving skills. We had plenty of time before we hit our first pub of eight. Buckled up, off we flew round familiar country roads that I had frequently driven. The car and my mate were loving it. Driving skills proven, we headed home to put the car away. That's when my mate piped up stating that he could drive just as good. Rattled by this unbelievable brag, I offered him the chance to prove it. We swapped seats. Same speed. Same confidence if not more. Same country roads. But unfamiliar to him. Attempting to corner a hair-pin bend, the red Ford Cortina 1.6 Ghia, now with only 23,007 miles on the clock, met its fate. Smashing into a stone gate pillar crumpling the stone wall of a cow field, the car came to a standstill. Smoke and steam billowed from the engine. The car was a right-off and doomed for the scrappy. Our eight pint pub crawl was cut short to last orders. And I have never forgotten making that adolescent dumbass decision to go for a drive.

Working in Soho Square, London at a large design company for a year as part of my degree course was an eye-opener. Not only was I working on amazing projects for large clients, I was working in an environment I had never dreamt of. Their work hard, play harder culture was drilled into my psyche for the rest of my career. It was the late eighties and life was fabulous in WC1- claimed to be the most creative square mile in the world. And we were paid very well even as an intern. Nowadays one is expected to work gratis on a year's placement. It was the norm to work sixty to eighty hour weeks, often until the early hours, but when we had achieved our goal, it was party time. Correction, pub time. We could see the pub from our design studio, The Nellie Dean. During heavy working weeks we would hit the pub at lunchtimes for an hour sinking Guinness as a substitute for food and continue grafting. During working evenings, takeaways from nearby restaurants were ordered for the teams. Cabs were booked to take you home safely ready for the next day. During the Summer weeks, a team of us represented the company in the Design Softball League. It was an unwritten rule, that these matches could not be missed because of the kudos of beating other competitive creative agencies. It wasn't just about winning games, it was about being the loudest, the most outrageous in the Edinburgh Castle Pub post match. This is where other creative companies would gain an insight into our company culture, which formed part of our recruitment strategy. Drinks of course, were claimed back on expenses. These weekly softball matches were the pinnacle of our week. Not only did I become close friends with people from our company, we all became friends with many others from our creative industry. However, one person in particular stood out. The girl from PR. I'd seen her a few times in our studio using the photocopier but did not have a chance or the courage to talk to her. Softball nights solved that. Following a great game, lots of laughter in the pub garden with a few tequila shots, we snogged in Regents Park. Secretively. Within a week I was invited round to hers for a bite to eat. The basement flat of a Victorian terraced house, where a famous psychologist had lived, as stated on the blue plaque on the wall. Whatever our relationship was or about to become, it was kept a secret from others at work. Not my decision. It made it more difficult when arranging to meet. London is so big you can be anonymous but you never know who's going to walk into the pub or restaurant and catch you out. We were both single. So what was the issue? I was the intern and she was the PR manager. People might talk, she kept saying. OK. I agreed. It was easier to eat at her place. The arrangement was for me to wait in the pub on the high street until she returned from work. Fine with me. She would walk past the pub window and I would see her. After five minutes I was to leave the pub, walk round the corner and knock on her flat door. Within an hour I had sunk three pints of Guinness and read the Evening Standard cover to cover and back to front. Another pint later, I began to think that I had missed her passing by. Bursting for the loo by now I went to the gents. The plan was to then go and knock on her door. Whilst trying to piss out four pints quickly holding my newspaper, disaster happened. I'd done a big splash fart. I heard someone come through the first door leading to the gents so I quickly ran into the cubicle. Undoing my white chinos, I checked my pants to see a pool of diarrhoea spilling onto the inside of my trousers. I'd properly shat my pants. The fear hit me. Why now! I panicked, kicked my shoes off and struggled out of my pants and trousers. The newspaper came in handy. The pants were then hidden in the bog brush holder. I awaited the bloke to leave before running to the sink for a handful of water and soap. I was a on the biggest date and I had fucked it up. Good and proper. Shit. And when I eventually knocked on her door, she wasn't in. I just sat at the bottom of the cast iron steps leading to her basement flat, head in hands. 'What's wrong with you?' she said, looking down upon me. My face told the story of utter shame and shock. I had to fess up. If I hadn't the relationship was dead. And

I would be in her eyes, the ultimate stink monster. My clothes were thrown in the washing machine, whilst I took a shower. I could hear her laughing in hysterics. The next day at work to avoid the chance of a trouser medallion in my now whiter than white chinos, I wore a pair of her french knickers. By the afternoon I'd forgotten, to the fun of my work colleagues who spotted them as we changed for softball.

Other dumbass memories came flooding back whilst staring at the fan in the kitchen. Like the time we gate-crashed the Design Awards at Grosvenor House Hotel. A huge annual black tie event where the industry celebrates the best work of the year. Tickets being scarce, two of us jumped in a black cab from our local pub opposite work, egging each other on to impose ourselves on our colleagues who were up for an award. Sat at the bar in the hotel lobby with a pint, we watched streams of waitresses with silver trays full of booze going through the double doors to the famous Great Room. One of London's largest and impressive halls with capacity for up to 2,000 guests. A shot of vodka and we were ready to make our grand entrance with the added drunken idea that it would be hilarious if we entered with our tops off. Bare chested we swung open the double doors and scanned the hundreds of tables full of smartly dressed guests. Unable to spot our friends we wandered through the sea of black ties as heads began to turn. The square and compasses symbol of Freemasonry was projected on the screen above the stage. The realisation that we had gate-crashed the wrong event in the wrong hall hit us like a coal shovel. All eyes on us as we legged it through the Great Room, dodging tables, out of the opposite door, down a maze of corridors, and out of a side door. Hyde Park Corner was rather cold at that time of night. Especially bare chested.

More drunk dumbass antics came to mind. I was on a roll of shame. Over the years the best nights were the ones when there's something memorable that stands out. It goes down as the night such and such happened and becomes easier for us all to remember and laugh about. Stumbling out of a club down Gerrard Street in Chinatown one particular night, I ended up covered in fish heads and maggot juice. For a laugh I climbed on the back of a dustbin lorry and sat there dangling my legs like a drunken Humpty Dumpty. One slip, and back I fell into the most foul rotting waste from the Chinese restaurants. Covered head to toe in slime, bits of offal and fish I climbed out with maggots wriggling on my clothes. I think of this dumbass event now as a near death experience. Imagine if the disposal mechanism was weight activated?

Work Summer parties always had a theme. This year was the White Party, held appropriately at a cricket ground in Highgate. Through peer pressure, I'd been convinced that this was the perfect setting to propose to my girlfriend. As word rapidly spread amongst my colleagues, the more I couldn't back out or bottle it. There I was, on stage peering into spotlights, as hundreds dressed in white starred in anticipation as the volume of the music softened. It was now or never. Not being able to identify my girlfriend in the crowd and looking into the abyss, I said those special words, on one knee. That was the straw that broke the camel's back. She moved out the next day.

The most embarrassing dumbass thing ever happened years later working for a large agency near Oxford Circus. A beautifully designed building with all the frills of a successful advertising agency, open plan studios on four floors with a bar and restaurant to entertain clients. It was originally designed for 500 employees but hard success had increased numbers by at least an additional two hundred, cramming us in like battery hens. It's not another toilet incident but more of a toilet paper dilemma. Somehow on exiting the loo, the toilet roll on the wall had caught on my clothing as I strode through the first packed studio, then the second towards the third without realising that a train of bog roll stretched the length of the whole floor. At my expense, I was the highlight of everyone's day, making it viral on social media. Dumbass.

THE MOUSE AND THE SILVER SHARK

As the sun rose over Cork, Ireland, Whiskers McGinn's nose twitched awake. The big mouse lived in an old shed near the waterfront and worked the nearby fishing boats scavenging for food along the pier and docks. He guarded his home from any intruders who wandered too close, mostly other rodents like himself.

Whiskers loved his world—the sounds of waves slapping against the old wooden pilings, the warm scent of engine oil that lingered on crates stacked by the warehouse, and the cool breeze that whispered through decaying stacks of newspapers. His days were spent exploring the city's nooks and crannies, looking for food, and avoiding the many dangers that urban life presented: cats, birds of prey, and humans. He was always full of energy and eager to explore a new sight or smell. For him, Cork was a place like no other. But he'd not known any other.

One day when he was taking shelter inside a massive blue steel container - a discarded container called 'Big Blue'. It had been unused in the dock for years. Whiskers discovered an enormous cruise ship had docked in the harbour during the night. Normally such ships would pass unnoticed by Whiskers; however this particular vessel was right next to Big Blue. It had eight decks and looked more like a floating town than a boat: bright lights sparkled along the edge of its deck where families strolled hand-in-hand. It had sailed across the Atlantic from New York and was docking for a few hours whilst passengers enjoyed the delights of Cork before the onward journey to the

Mediterranean. Whiskers couldn't resist creeping aboard just to get a taste of what sea travel might be like.

The smell of raw fish permeated everything along the portside but was tempered by seagull excrement wafting into the air. As his nose got used to it, he decided it wasn't so bad after all. A crow landed with a squawk and strutted towards him in full view, its head bobbing up and down, then back again in jerky movements, while it eyed him warily. Whiskers hastened past it, towards a chain that secured the liner to the dock. Then scurried along the huge chain easily enough, through a round hole where the mechanism winds it back onto the deck. Once aboard, Whiskers slowly looked up. Affixed on the wall in front of him, glistening in shiny brass letters, was the liner's name SILVER SHARK.

Whiskers ventured from the top deck and began exploring the ship's many amenities and activities. Scurrying past glamorous passengers everywhere. Whiskers had to be discreet so as not to get noticed. Crew, dressed in pristine, pressed, white uniforms were at hand to every beck and call. Elegantly carrying fresh linen and towels, others cocktails and champagne, lobsters and fillet steak. Whiskers had never seen anything like it.

The mouse became increasingly adept at navigating his new world. He quickly learnt to utilise his surroundings to his advantage by turning up at certain kitchens knowing full well the staff were too busy to notice him, sneaking into lockers set aside for uniforms, avoiding metal grates that were food waste disposal, tipped directly into the sea, watching acrobats practice during the day, and eavesdropping on interesting conversations (and making note of which staff member's or passenger's door he needs to sneak beneath most often).

Passengers began to return to the liner after experiencing Cork, some a little unsteady after a guided tour around Jamesons Whiskey Distillery. A few singing old American songs as they embarked, laden with cases of Irish Whiskey. The liner was destined to set off from Cork harbour later that night. Next port of call was Seville, Spain, where they'll be docking for two days. Within a few hours the ship's horn blew, the late passengers were aboard, and then they were off. Slowly creating ripples and waves in the sea, as they headed steadily for the Mediterranean. Lights from hundreds of port holes and windows of the Silver Shark could be seen in the distance, until the liner disappeared out of sight.

On one of his runs, Whiskers encountered passenger Lucy Willows, playing a game of Black Jack with other male passengers in the casino. She was holding court and they kept smiling at her trying to hold her attention. Whiskers was drawn to her warm personality. Although Lucy was unaware of his presence, Whiskers heard snippets of her conversations with passengers about the importance of being discreet. Later, as Whiskers observed, Lucy would visit them in their cabins, and perform whatever acts they paid for. Lucy, one of many on-board hookers, makes thousands of dollars a day, paid to her in gambling chips from the casino. Whiskers thought this was a very clever, very discreet way of payment. Untraceable. Just like himself, hiding in the shadows. Keeping a low profile, whilst scavenging for five star delicacies throughout the dining rooms and kitchens. Often outside cabins, left on trays. Later that night, Whiskers saw Lucy Willows knock on the cabin door of a slimy looking, middle aged man dressed in his towelling robe, smelling of aftershave from the duty free shop. Lucy, left in under an hour, smelling of that same aftershave.

As the voyage went on, the entertainment on the liner became more daring. Whiskers particularly enjoyed watching late night rehearsals of different shows with performers perfecting their craft, unaware that a mouse was hiding within the curtains or nestled up to piles of sweaty garments. One evening, Whiskers sneaked into a show where the only light shone from red dots on the floor guiding passengers to their movie-theatre style seats. A neon sign occasionally flickered "Adults Only" as the music started and the curtains rose. The set resembled a French wartime brothel, with girls entering in time with the melody while stripping down to their suspenders, stockings, and half-cut bras. When they reached the centre of the stage they found a group of American soldiers ready to choose a girl and take part in an all-encompassing live sex act. At first, audience members whistled and cheered but then soon fell silent as things got hotter.

Whiskers felt the surge of water against the hull, and caught a whiff of salt air. His whiskers twitched enthusiastically. This was all very familiar; he had been on this ship before--but that seemed like such a long time ago. Now it was his second home. Whiskers' adventures onboard, led him to cross paths with Hunter Finch, the crew member responsible for maintaining a rodent-free environment. Hunter was relentless in his pursuit of Whiskers (or so Whiskers thought) setting traps and using poison to try and catch him. Whiskers used all his newfound knowledge and skills to outsmart Hunter, and avoid capture. Every so often when danger loomed exceptionally close, an involuntary chill ran through his tiny body and induced a shiver that sent his whiskers bouncing about madly. He loved playing tricks on Hunter Finch, but feared being near him too much to get playful. The great expanse shouldered by the Silver Shark stretched as far as the eye could see, seemingly without an end in sight.

Whiskers, now becoming the ship's resident mouse, sensed danger from Hunter and kept a wary eye on him. Listening intently through an air vent located in Hunter's cabin, Whiskers overheard a rather cryptic conversation about a passenger and "the action" that was set to take place that night at 2am on the upper deck by the swimming pool. The little mouse knew exactly where that was. Intrigued by what he had heard, Whiskers scampered along the ship's upper deck and hid behind a pile of towels near the pool, waiting for 2am to arrive.

The night was dark with only sporadic spotlights casting beams of light across the water. The moonlight reflected off the sea's surface creating shimmering patterns on the waves that lapped against the bow of the liner. Despite the calm surroundings, the ballroom, cabarets, and casinos were thriving with passengers hell-bent on having a good time. Whiskers could smell the fresh saltwater air as he waited patiently for something to happen.

Suddenly he spotted a man dressed in black tie carrying a heavy briefcase. Hunter appeared just seconds later, and although Whiskers couldn't hear their words, he could tell from their body language that something sinister was about to occur. As soon as the man opened his briefcase, Hunter's face lit up with greed. The briefcase was placed on the deck and the man opened his palm as if to receive something from Hunter. But instead of handing anything over, Hunter pulled out a knife and plunged it into the man's chest. The man let out a bloodcurdling scream that couldn't be heard from inside, before being shoved overboard by Hunter without hesitation.

Whiskers had just witnessed a murder unfold before his eyes and watched as Hunter calmly picked up the briefcase and walked away from the gruesome scene without looking back. If Whiskers thought his time onboard the Silver Shark was overdue, he knew for sure now that it was time to leave.

On his return to the lower decks, Whiskers saw a man being arrested by three crewmen. He had been accused of cheating at cards and was being taken to the ship's cell in the lowest deck hidden away deep in the hull. On the corridor leading to passenger's cabins, a large guy wearing a Rolex watch slapped his younger wife. He was accusing her of flirting with a crew member. He was just a jealous rich husband who had married an ex-model, more than half his age, and struggled to cope with any advances on her. She didn't react, just looked him in the eye, as make-up tricked down her face. This had happened many times before. This had been a night Whiskers would never forget.

In the morning whilst scavenging for food, Whiskers' ears perked up as he eavesdropped on Captain O'Malley and Chef Gustave's conversation about the importance of hygiene in the kitchen. The Captain was complaining about having food poisoning. Chef Gustave argued that it wasn't from anything he had served from his kitchen that he was crazy thinking that it was his fault.

The breakfast lounge was full of the smells of freshly cooked food. A father sat with his girl at a table in the corner, absentmindedly stroking her hair. However, Whiskers had learnt otherwise whilst prowling around the cabins he had overheard the girl questioning the man. She was asking whether he was going to dump her once back in New York in his ivory tower, like he had done with all the other personal secretaries before her that he had seduced then fired before her. It was all a facade of deep lies, a pretence to hide from everyone that he was having a multitude of relationships outside his marriage. The girl's eyes were downcast and she nibbled on toast, lost in thought.

In a few hours time, the liner would be docking at Seville. Whiskers wanted to feast on himself before docking. He was unaware what Seville was like and where his next meal was coming from. As he entered Chef Gustave's kitchen through a gap in the grille, he could hear the chef muttering under his breath as he laid out pâtés, slices of rich meat drizzled with sauce, small fowl cut into tiny pieces smothered in herbs and spices, sautéed vegetables shimmering with oils and butter, and other tantalising dishes on a silver tray. It smelled like a dream. Captain O'Malley had the dining room all to himself as he savoured his meal- unaware that Chef Gustave had added a pinch of Thallium.

With land in sight, and only a couple of hours until the liner was due to dock in Seville, Whiskers reflected on his adventure on the Silver Shark. He knew his time on board had been eye opening and shocking at times but it was all part of life's journey.

Lucy Willows, the seemingly innocent hooker, was earning $10K every day.

Hunter, the notorious hit man who had killed on order from some of the most influential people in corporate businesses, was cold-hearted and lonely.

A billionaire that had a tendency to become over-jealous when men approached his younger wife - money could not buy him love.

The cheating husband hired a new personal assistant at work each year and groomed them to sleep with him - would this be the last time?

A gambler blessed with a photographic memory, he gambled in casinos until he got banned for counting cards.

Strippers performed for pay ten times what they would make on shore. Many were students taking advantage of the summertime or gap years to fund their education.

The Chef was driven to poisoning because his lover, the Captain, had become bored with their steady relationship and preferred hopping around with younger toy boys.

The cruise liner finally reached its destination in the Mediterranean and Whiskers realised that this was his chance to escape from the Silver Shark. He must be unwavering and take decisive action; there can be no more errors. His breathing became heavy as he made his way through the vessel, keeping himself hidden using all the methods he had learnt. Clambering back through the hole, onto the dock of Seville, and then up the long chain, he felt a wave of relief wash over him as the sun began to rise slowly above the horizon and freedom welcomed him ashore. It reminded him of his hometown dock in Cork but it was much larger. Soon enough, Whiskers will know his way around here too.

His adventure continues.